An Aberrant Mind

Ken MacGregor

Sirens Call Publications

An Aberrant Mind

Copyright © 2014 Ken MacGregor
Licensed to and Distributed by Sirens Call Publications [2014]
www.sirenscallpublications.com

Print Edition; First Edition

Edited by Gloria Bobrowicz

Cover Design © Sirens Call Publications

ISBN-13: 978-0615995687 (Sirens Call Publications)
ISBN-10: 0615995683

For Gabriel and Maggie who aren't allowed to read this book until they're much older.

AN ABERRANT MIND

Acknowledgements

Thanks to (Brian) Poploski for so many, many ideas.

Thanks to Scott Hatkow for the bagel challenge.

Thanks to my patient, understanding, supportive wife Liz Dahl MacGregor for not killing me in my sleep.

Also, thank you to everyone who was kind enough to read my stories and offer feedback and encouragement.

Thanks to Gloria, Nina and Julianne at Sirens Call Publications for taking a chance on me when I had no idea what I was doing and sticking with me as I figured it out. I'm still learning, but I stumble less frequently these days.

Sirens Call Publicatons

Introduction

I don't think you realize exactly what you're holding in your hot little hands. In fact, I'm absolutely certain of it. Yes, this is a collection of short fiction. Yes, some guy named Ken MacGregor wrote it. Yes, you've seen it all… blah, blah, blah. Have you heard the stories of the *Necronomicon*? How the Mad Arab, Abdul Alhazred created a tome that invoked the Elder Gods and how the book has landed at the feet of the desperate and powerless throughout history and changed the course of events. THAT is what you hold in your hands here.

I do not mean to infer that you are desperate and powerless.

Or that MacGregor is a Mad Arab.

But when in Rome…

Books can be dangerous and not just the Lovecraftian ones, either. How much blood has been spilled to keep the contents of books a secret? How many lives have been snuffed out because a book told a group of bloodthirsty zealots to do it? Books are powerful, people. Books are weapons. Books are dangerous.

Which brings us back full circle and to An Aberrant Mind.

The stories that fill this tome are fantastical. Tales of zombies and killer bagels, vengeful squirrels and succubi prove that MacGregor's imagination is alive and well. When we dig deeper, though, that is when things get a little disturbing.

When we examine what MacGregor is REALLY saying, the artist as auteur comes alive. The message of these stories, the themes that permeate and infect us, are much more than the sum of the parts. Excellent pacing, clever dialogue and intriguing plotlines, when added together, usually become an effective story… but there is so much more here. Like that Mad Arab, or the architects of parables, the sum total of these stories is more than a fun, if horrific, collection. It is a statement.

The sneaky part is that MacGregor gets into the heart of the story quickly, punches the reader in the face, and moves him or her along to the next story so fast that you don't know that you have been *affected*, or infected, by what he was trying to say.

In so doing, Ken MacGregor says many things in these stories, but it is the theme of powerlessness and loss and desperation that rings so true throughout. His characters make the right choices. His characters are true to themselves and the worlds that our intrepid author has crafted around them and, in that, not only is the fantastic made real, but the theme and message of the stories are *inevitable*. That means there is a truth in here beyond the fiction. And it hurts. And it is necessary.

And, dear God, MacGregor revels in it. He is most definitely a sadist and his tortures don't end with his characters. They need to make horrible, life-changing decisions. A sick little brother needs mercy and an extreme case of noctophobia alters the lives of many. Even multiple visits with Gavin, our globe-hopping lycanthrope are filled with terrible, awful choices. Monsters are, indeed, real but not just in these pages. Their creator is equally as monstrous and because of this the reader is victim to his sadism.

If these stories were poorly written, MacGregor would get a pass from me. If there were no wit, or even an iota of literary merit, then we, as readers, could overlook the damage he inflicts on unsuspecting characters and towns. But that just doesn't happen.

We care. God damn him, we care about these people and what happens to them. Trust me, it isn't pretty. What MacGregor has done is simple and effective: he has penned full, round characters that engage us emotionally and then he makes them do awful things. Terrible things.

What is the worst part? I will tell you.

He likes it.

David C. Hayes
Winter 2014

Ken MacGregor

A CREATURE STIRRING

Julian set down several bags of presents and unlocked his apartment. He lived on the top floor of a nineteen story building; his floor had eight apartments. Julian opened his door, and was hit by a smell, strong, sharp and musky, wild and strange.

Julian dragged in the bags and searched his apartment, turning on all the lights. He found nothing. Probably, an animal got into the ventilation shaft and died. He poured himself a glass of Merlot and sat on the couch to wrap the first present. It was a toy unicorn, white, with a gold mane, tail and horn. It was ten inches tall. Julian's sister, Alice had two girls, Georgia and Nell. Nell was going to explode when she opened this.

Julian had learned how to wrap presents neatly from an ex-girlfriend. Sara was an artist, beautiful, creative, smart. He was infatuated with her. But, she was neurotic. It didn't last. Sara wrapped presents like the professionals at the fancy stores, all perfect corners and flat sides.

Julian finished his wine and stretched his back. Half the bottle was gone, and half the presents were done. Suddenly, Julian heard something moving over his head.

He looked up at the vent in the drop ceiling. He couldn't see anything from the floor, so he dragged one of the kitchen barstools over and climbed on it. It was dark in there, but Julian thought he saw something moving. He studied it, hoping his eyes would adjust to the darkness. He raised himself on his toes, cocking his head to look through the slats.

Bang! Something hit the vent right above his face; he fell off the stool, more embarrassed than hurt.

"Fuck!" He yelled. "Bastard." Julian gave the vent the finger.

Julian sat back down on the couch. He poured another glass and drank some. He looked at the remaining presents and scowled. He had lost interest in wrapping.

Julian drank some more wine, and glared up at the vent. Stupid animal. The smell was getting worse in here, too. Have to call the super.

Julian finished the wine in his glass, a little buzzed. He got up and went to his bedroom. He peeled off his clothes and crawled into bed, trying not to think about the animal in his ceiling. He was drifting off when he heard movement. He opened his eyes and glowered at the ceiling.

"Seriously? You're following me? Give me a break." Julian pulled the covers over his head. A few seconds later, he pulled them down. The scratching was louder now. Julian sat up, the blanket sliding down to his waist. The light was off; it was hard to see. He sat very still in his bed and listened.

He heard it again. Julian grabbed the bedside lamp and turned it on, pointing it at the ceiling.

He watched, heart thudding in his chest. In the ceiling, the vent cover dropped half an inch. Julian gasped. Then, it was pulled back up suddenly. Julian scooted back to the headboard, keeping the light trained up there.

The vent cover exploded down out of the ceiling, along with drywall fragments and dust.

"Aah!" Julian screamed. He trained the light on the floor, but there was just the metal vent cover, one corner bent from the fall. Julian got off the bed and held the lamp like a sword. He took three steps, felt a small tug from the lamp and the light went out.

"Shit!" Julian dove across the bed for the other lamp. He did not want to be in the dark. He was almost there when something thudded to the floor. He froze, listening. Julian could hear breathing. The musky smell filled his nostrils.

Slowly, he felt for the other lamp, edging his body across the bed. His fingers found the bedside table, then the base of the lamp, and finally the switch. Behind him, something climbed onto the bed. Something heavy. The bed springs creaked, protesting the weight.

Julian was scared as hell, but he had to know.

The light came on, and Julian looked. The thing was long and sinuous with six short legs and a massive head. It looked like something out of mythology; some dark god's pet. From its mouth came a large, black tongue, not forked, but like a human tongue, only longer. It licked Julian, tasting his chest. The saliva made his skin tingle and burn.

"Please," Julian said to it. "It's Christmas. For god's sake, please."

A buzzing invaded his head, an angry wasp's nest in his brain. He heard/felt/thought a voice.

"Beg me," it said. "For your life."

"Please don't kill me," Julian said. "I'll do anything. Please."

The beast pushed Julian down, pinning him to the bed with its weight. It lay across him, its face inches from his own. It looked into Julian's eyes. Its eyes were gold; they caught the light and it swirled in their depths. Julian saw intelligence, and hunger in those eyes. Even so, they were beautiful. Its mouth stretched, and with horror, Julian realized it was smiling.

***

Julian grabbed the eight bags by the handles, pulled them out, and closed the trunk with his elbow. He walked up the path to Alice's front door. She, having seen him coming opened it right away. Julian grinned at her behind his sunglasses. She grinned right back.

"Merry Christmas, big brother," she said, hugging him awkwardly between the bags.

"Merry Christmas to you," Julian replied. He stepped inside and put down the bags. His nieces came running up for hugs, and he grabbed them both at once.

"Can I get you something?" Alice asked him. Julian nodded and followed her to the kitchen. "Coffee, maybe?"

Julian smiled at his sister, took off his shades and gazed at her with his gold eyes. He licked his lips with his long, black tongue. Alice felt an awful buzzing sensation in her mind.

"Beg me," he said to her. "For your life."

THE ABDUCTION
OF GLYNNIS JOHNSON

Glynnis Johnson had always wanted to retire to Florida, despite the cliché. She had taught third grade in Michigan since time immemorial and had a tidy nest egg put away. Glynnis was quite happy to turn her back on winter for the remainder of her years.

Glynnis purchased a small house in a nice neighborhood just a few blocks from the ocean. Close enough to walk, so she did, daily. She liked to stand at the water's edge and gaze out at the vast blue. The Great Lakes were nice, in the summer, but this - this was something else. Standing there, she could feel the *immensity* of the sea. She loved it.

Glynnis had moved in September, the very day she would have returned to the school in previous years. The movers drove the truck down, and she drove her own car, a Crown Victoria; she had been buying that kind of car since they started making them back in '55, when she got her first one for her 18th birthday. In all that time, she had never had an accident or a speeding ticket. She still drove, and relished the trip south behind the wheel of her dependable Detroit steel.

Glynnis stayed in a hotel overnight; it was a long drive and at 75 she wasn't up to doing it all at once. She left early after the continental breakfast and got to her new house in the afternoon. The movers had set up her furniture and stacked the boxes neatly along the walls by room. It was nice to see professionalism. Once she unpacked her laptop, she went back to their website to leave a positive review.

Her first months in Florida were wonderful, and Glynnis made new friends quickly; it was easy, as everyone was her age and had also lived in Michigan or neighboring states. She found three to play Euchre within a month and they played every Tuesday. But, it was the sea she loved most. It drew her, a moth to flame, and she stood on the shore every day, unless the weather was a beast.

Then something odd happened.

It started as a tiny aberration, and Glynnis only became aware of the difference because she stood in the same spot day after day. Way out there, well beyond the bright red buoy was what looked like a small island. Which would be fine if not for the fact there hadn't been one there before. She wondered if she had spent too much time in the sun. Glynnis decided not to worry about it, and not to mention it to her Tuesday Euchre group, though they talked about pretty much everything. Something about it made her keep it to herself.

Glynnis couldn't help wondering if maybe this was a sign of early onset of dementia. She felt perfectly lucid, but would she know the difference? If one is losing one's mind, would one notice? Scary thought.

On subsequent trips to the beach, the island grew ever bigger. Glynnis watched, fascinated as it grew out of the ocean. She brought binoculars with her to study this bizarre phenomenon: the island appeared to be yellow or green, or some combination. It was not a healthy color. It was not smooth, but textured, with shrubs or hillocks all over, though there did not appear to be anything as grand as a tree. In her analytic teacher's mind, she wondered: a. how an island could be visibly rising from the sea, and b. why she had heard nothing about it on the news nor seen it in the paper. None of her friends mentioned it either, and Glynnis knew for a fact that some of them spent a great deal of time at the beach.

"Perhaps," she said to herself, binoculars glued to her eyes, "I'm going crazy after all."

"You're not," said a voice next to her, startling her. "It's real." Glynnis turned to the dead man standing next to her. He was naked, gray and bloated, a drowning victim. He belched and the smell was unbearable. Glynnis gagged and her heart beat against her ribcage.

"Excuse me," the corpse said. "I came to tell you that He's coming for you. I have no idea why, but you're somehow special. He almost never makes a trip out of the water. Frankly, I'm a little jealous." The walking dead man looked at his wrist, though he wore no watch. "Look at the time! I have to get back. Be ready."

His rotten backside twitched as he walked away, lichen and barnacles clustered on the left cheek. Glynnis watched, fascinated and repulsed in equal parts. While she did, her mind raced. *He's coming for me? He never leaves the water? Who is he, that he sends drowning victims out of the water to announce his intentions? And just what are those intentions? For that matter, why am I the only on the beach who saw that happen?*

It was that last thought that cemented the idea that Glynnis was, in fact going insane. Once home, she made an appointment with a psychiatrist; she found one in the yellow pages. He had an opening in two weeks; she hoped that would be soon enough. Out loud, she thanked his receptionist and hung up.

The next day, despite misgivings that bordered on actual fear, Glynnis found herself back at the beach, binoculars in tow. The island, if that's what it was, was noticeably larger today. It was the size of Oahu now; it made her think of a lovely vacation spent there with her late husband two or three lifetimes ago. A ridge was now visible on the edge facing the beach; it ran most of the length of the island, but it disappeared in the middle and was most prominent on either side of that gap. There was something familiar about that shape, but Glynnis couldn't put her finger on it.

Suddenly, she realized she was knee deep in the ocean. Glynnis had not been aware of walking forward; she had not felt the cool water until it was over her calves, getting her dress wet. Pulling the binoculars away from her face, Glynnis stared at the island. What is happening to me, she thought. I mustn't come back here again. She went home, changed clothes and fixed herself a Tom Collins; Glynnis wasn't much of a drinker, but this seemed like a very good time for a drink. She went to bed early, but the disquiet of her mind would not let her sleep. At 1am, she gave up. Glynnis made a pot of coffee and listened to it brew. When it was finished, she poured a cup and added milk and one scoop of sugar. Glynnis stopped in mid-stir.

"Good lord," she said aloud. Glynnis had finally recognized the shape of that island ridge. "Eyebrows."

Preposterous, Glynnis thought, angry with the absurdity of it all. Abandoning her cup, she pulled on her long coat, proof against the cool wind of Florida evenings. Glynnis grabbed a flashlight and walked to the beach. In the houses, only porch lights and night-lights were on. When she arrived, she found her spot, alone on the public beach.

"All right," she called. "You wanted me. I'm here. Goodness knows I'm probably just an old lady in the early stages of dementia, alone on a beach, talking to an island that only exists in my mind, but I want to see how this plays out, and I'm losing my patience. So, if you are out there, and listening, I'm ready for whatever you have in mind. Though, God only knows what you'd want with a retired school teacher."

Nothing happened for almost a minute, which was enough time for Glynnis to feel quite foolish and go home. As she turned to leave, she heard the ocean move. It was an *immense* sound. Glynnis looked back to see the tide retreating from her, faster than she thought possible. She glanced up and her breath caught. The 'island' was rising from the water at an astonishing rate, though it was clear now that this was no island at all, but a figure of impossible proportions. What had been visible was just the top of its head. As the creature's face broke the water, eyes the size of sports arenas, the water reversed course and began pounding the beach. Glynnis tried to run, backward, unwilling to take her own eyes off the monster, lest it grab and eat her. The ocean let her get a few steps before sweeping her away. She took a quick breath and held it. Glynnis hit something hard enough to crack a rib and reached out. She caught hold of whatever she hit and held on for her life, her chest screaming from the twin pains of the fracture and air held overlong. But, as she knew it would, the sea reversed course again and tried to drag her with it. Glynnis did not let go, adrenaline and terror turning her seventy-five-year-old arms into iron. The water was gone, just like that, and she inhaled sweet, salty air, grateful despite the sudden pain breathing now caused. Have to have that looked at, she thought. Then she remembered the greater threat.

The horror from the deep was fully erect now, towering thousands of feet over the surface. Glynnis thanked God it was too dark to see clearly, but she could still make out enough. Under those enormous eyes, its face spread outward in dozens of tentacles, each roughly the size of the Huron River back home. Her mind rebelled. Glynnis prayed. She begged for it to stop. She panicked, but what she did not do was let go of that parking meter.

The drowned man was back, slightly more barnacle laden now. He squatted next to her, his flaccid genitals two feet from her face. A tiny crab nestled in the hair, flexing its claws in the air. Glynnis thought, absurdly, *he has crabs*, and she laughed, but it came out more like a choking sob.

"I have made peace with *my* god," the naked corpse said to her. "Have you with yours? If not, now would be a good time."

"You be quiet," Glynnis said. "You are a figment of my imagination, and I'd like you to go away."

"Sorry" the drowned man said, "Can't do that. My Master awaits your pleasure. And, pleasure it will be: immortality, power, riches, everything awaits you in R'lyeh. Also, the opportunity to adore His Greatness up close and personal. You have no idea how lucky you are to be chosen. I'd give up any two limbs to be you."

"Go ahead," Glynnis said, smiling. "I won't stop you."

"I admire your spirit! Like a Viking, dying with a joke on your lips. His Immensity will like you, I am sure."

"Please tell your *god*," Glynnis said, "that I am not interested. I retired to Florida so I could have peace and quiet and no longer have to put up with white cold in the air and black ice on the roads. I have taught third graders for forty-seven years, and I can tell you with authority that not only are they more frightening than you, but they frequently smell worse. I am not an easily intimidated woman, sir, and I will not be led off to some watery grave with some enormous being out of some perverse society's mythology. Not quietly anyway. I intend to fight for my life and my freedom until I have lost every shred of both, and after that, I will still scream and kick and flail, taking down everyone and everything I can with me when I go. So, Mr. Bloated Corpse, you go ahead and give it your best shot, because I do not fear you or your monster."

The dead man just stared at her for several seconds, then he grinned and clapped his hands, lauding Glynnis with damp applause.

"That," he said, "was a lovely speech. Moving, heartfelt and filled with righteous indignation. Brava, good lady, brava. And, were I the compassionate sort, whose conscience could override the directive of his god, I would surely let you go. But, I'm not."

And, with that, he pried her hands loose from the meter as if they were cooked pasta and carried Glynnis into the sea. True to her word, she fought as hard as she could, but never had a chance. As her breath ran out, she panicked, but when her lungs filled with water, she found that not only could she still breathe, but that her ribs no longer hurt. In fact, she felt none of the usual aches and discomforts that come with age. Glynnis was completely pain free for the first time in years.

Well, Glynnis thought. *I must be dead. That's all right, then*. She noticed she was still being led deeper into the ocean by the drowning victim. Glynnis looked at him. He was smiling to himself, a man happy to be going home. He caught her eye.

"It's nice, huh?" he said. "Quiet down here. I love it."

Glynnis had to nod. It was nice to be away from the cars and planes and TVs and chatter. They walked on in surprisingly companionable silence. Glynnis was no longer afraid; she knew she was either mad or dead, so was prepared for anything. Glynnis still had no idea why she was here or what to expect, but, physically, she felt better than she had in years, and she approached the disturbing, chaotic architecture of R'lyeh with something like optimism.

A LESSON LEARNED

FROM ARCHIE

Jeremy looked at his mom through teary eyes. Between them, Archie lay on the floor with his eyes closed, breathing in sporadic rasps.

"What's wrong with him, Mom?" Jeremy asked. Last week, Archie had run around the yard with Jeremy, trying to grab the chew toy out of his hand. Jeremy had laughed and ran all over, the yellow lab bumping against him again and again. Now, he was like a different dog.

"Archie is sick, honey" Jeremy's mom held his shoulders. "The vet said he's not going to get better. I'm sorry." Tears fell from her eyes, though her voice was steady. Sympathetic tears sprang from Jeremy's eyes. He never could stand to see his mother cry.

"Is he hurting?" Jeremy asked.

"I'm afraid he is," his mom whispered.

"What do we do?" Jeremy asked. "How do we make it better for him?"

"Honey," his mom said. "We need to put Archie to sleep."

"What does that mean?"

"We have to help him pass away," his mom said. "It's the only way to stop him from suffering, and he's going to die anyway." Over the dog, Jeremy hugged his mom, tears falling freely now, both snuffling and sobbing.

"How?" Jeremy asked, when he could talk.

"Your father is going to take Archie out to the woods. He'll shoot him and bury him. When it's all over, you can go visit the grave, okay?"

"Dad's going to *shoot* Archie?" Jeremy was shocked.

"Honey," his mom said. "It's the merciful thing to do. The dog is in pain all the time, and this will end it."

"I guess," Jeremy said. "If you think Archie will be better off. You do, right?"

"Of course," his mom said. "Your dad wouldn't do it if there was any other way. We all love Archie, honey. We don't want him to suffer anymore."

***

Four years later, Jeremy, ten now, still visited Archie's grave every couple months. He went there to think, to be alone. They talked about getting another dog, but his mom got pregnant, and then had Simon and they never got around to it. Simon was three now and almost never left Jeremy's side. Simon followed Jeremy to visit Archie sometimes, when Jeremy let him. He told his little brother about the dog, about how much Jeremy loved him and missed him still. Jeremy showed Simon pictures of Archie in albums, on the fridge and on the computer. Simon started bugging their parents about getting a dog. Once again, they said they'd think about it, but Jeremy didn't think they wanted to. He wasn't sure he wanted to, either; no dog could ever replace Archie.

In October, Simon got sick. He had pneumonia and couldn't get out of bed. The normally high-energy pre-schooler was a feverish lump. Jeremy's parents were frantic with worry. On the third day of Simon's illness, Jeremy went in to talk to him.

"How you feeling, little guy?" Jeremy smiled at his brother.

"Not good," Simon said. "Hot."

"You'll be okay," Jeremy said. "You'll get better soon. You'll see."

"I won't," Simon said. "I'm always gonna be sick." Jeremy stared at his brother. That would be awful. He stroked Simon's hair away from his burning forehead. Simon closed his eyes. His chest rose and fell in ragged gasps. Jeremy kept his hand on Simon's head as tears fell down his cheeks. He couldn't stand to see his little brother suffer.

That night, when his parents were asleep, Jeremy got out of bed and pulled on a pair of jeans. He pulled the key from the little ridge beneath his father's desk and opened the cabinet he was never supposed to touch. Jeremy slipped on his shoes and tiptoed back to his room. Simon was fast asleep, still hot to the touch, still trying to get enough air. Jeremy shook his head at the sadness of a little kid so sick. He picked his brother up in his arms and carried him outside. Jeremy nudged the door shut behind him with his foot and walked with his burden into the woods.

At Archie's grave, Jeremy set Simon down on the leaves. Simon gave a sleepy groan.

"Sh," Jeremy said. "It's going to be better soon, little guy." He pulled his father's pistol from his belt and loaded the bullets into the chambers. Crying freely now, Jeremy put the barrel to his little brother's forehead. Simon's eyes opened and blinked a few times.

"Where are we?" He asked his brother.

21

"Out by Archie," Jeremy said, his voice catching on sobs.

"Why?"

"I'm going to put you to sleep," Jeremy said. "You don't have to be sick anymore. I love you."

"I love you, too."

Jeremy squeezed the trigger with a thunderous bang and did the merciful thing.

SeaWolf

Gavin always said if he got turned into a werewolf, he'd kill himself.

The very last time he said those words, he was nineteen, across the state line in the bar with a fake ID that said he was twenty-three. He was well on his way to impressing the half-Chinese girl by the dartboards, and was feeling the three beers he'd already had; it was a nice, pleasant hum that promised to get louder as the night went on. The girl said her name was Ariel, "like the mermaid" and he said no: like the sprite in Shakespeare's 'The Tempest' and she lit up. As long as he didn't piss her off somehow, Gavin was definitely getting in this girl's pants.

Then, as it often does, the conversation came around to werewolves. Four new ones were spotted in this county alone and a whole lot more suspected. Now, people will tolerate a werewolf, as long as it sticks to eating wild animals; hell, they'll even overlook the occasional loss of livestock on the farm. But, at the first human casualty, they form a posse and hunt that bastard down. Every man among them carries a rifle, a pistol and a silver knife. You shoot a werewolf enough times, it's down for a long time before it can heal enough to fight back. And silver, well, that shit works.

So, naturally when the bar got around to the werewolf talk, Gavin said what he always says.

"Good," said a man at the bar without turning around. "Save us some trouble then, boy."

"You ever kill a werewolf, buddy?" Gavin was annoyed that this man pulled attention away from him; he was especially irritated by the way Ariel was sizing the guy up.

"Five." An impressed murmur went through the room. Gavin was impressed despite himself. Five werewolves! He was either lucky or very, very good. Maybe both.

"How'd you do it?" someone asked.

"It's different every time," the man said, "No two are alike. Some are cunning, some ferocious, some just plain stupid. Just like other people." He looked at Gavin, who flushed, not sure if he was being insulted or not.

"So, when your turn comes," the man went on, Gavin noting the use of when and not if, "you do just that: find a nice sharp silver knife and open up your veins. And don't put it off; no dilly-dallying on the way to your suicide, boy."

"My name is Gavin."

"Mine's Cornelius. I'll make you an offer, Gavin: if you don't have the balls to do it yourself, you come to me, and I'll be happy to do it for you. No charge. Public service you know."

This got a few laughs from the bar. Ariel seemed to lose interest in Gavin; in fact, she was heading toward Cornelius. Gavin turned away from them and took a long pull from his beer. Behind him, he could hear them talk.

"I'm Ariel."

"Like the mermaid," he said back. "I like your tail."

Ariel laughed and Gavin cringed inside. Fuck this, he thought. I'm outta here. He finished his beer in a few swallows and grabbed his jacket. He flew through the door, nearly hitting a pretty blonde and her date with it.

"Sorry," he mumbled and shrank into his coat. The wind had picked up and it must have dropped fifteen degrees while he was inside. He kept his head down and looked for his car in the parking lot. Damn it! Where the hell did he park? Oh yeah, right, backed in to the spot, way over by the edge so nobody would notice the out-of-state plates. When you live this close to the border, using the fake ID over in Jersey is just common sense.

Gavin fumbled for his keys, but he couldn't remember which pocket they were in. He tossed around a few choice expletives and ran his hands through his pockets again, faster this time, as if that would somehow help. Finally, he remembered they were in his jacket pocket, not his pants and he pulled them out triumphantly.

"Ta-Da!" he announced to no one. Hand still high in the air, holding the keys, Gavin froze. He heard something. It was close. A low, throaty, animal growl that made his bowels weak and his mind panic. *Run!* His mind screamed at him. *Run, you fool!* But he couldn't move. Couldn't even lower his hand. He was stuck like that, and suddenly he understood why they called it 'petrified'. This only lasted maybe two seconds, and then Gavin's muscles started to work again. He ran for the car. It was only about twenty feet. He could make it. He hit the button on the remote to open the doors, hit it again to open them all without knowing why and ran as fast as he could for that car.

He almost made it.

***

When he woke up, Gavin hurt. He hurt more than ever before in his life, and that's including the time he fell out of a tree in fifth grade and one of his ribs broke, piercing his lung. And, god, that hurt! That felt like a giant bamboo spike had been shoved through his chest and left there for five days. This was worse. Pieces of Gavin were missing. He could see some of them, but others were gone forever, being digested, no doubt by whatever attacked him. He still had his left arm, completely intact somehow, but his right arm was gone from the elbow down, and both legs were shredded, though still attached. His face was ripped, he could feel it. There were deep furrows elsewhere, too, caused by enormous claws and rending teeth. I am not in a good way, he thought to himself. But, he was alive, and he clung to that. He pulled himself with his good arm toward his car. He almost managed to get to the door when he blacked out. Or maybe he died. He had no idea. He didn't really care.

***

This time, when Gavin woke up, he felt a whole lot better. In fact, he'd never felt better in his life. He opened his eyes to an unfamiliar room, white walls, sunshine coming in through the thin curtains, a tray set out with breakfast. He was ravenous, so he ate. The food was mostly gone when Gavin noticed he was eating with his right hand. The hand that, last he knew, was torn - bitten - off. He stopped eating and looked at it. The skin was pink, hairless and soft, like a baby's. He was still staring at it when the door opened.

"Ah, good. You're one of the quick healers. That makes it easier, usually. How do you feel?"

"I'm great. Who the hell are you?"

"I," said the well-dressed man of about 50, "am your patron, your mentor, your guide. Your Sherpa if you like; feel free to choose your own title. I'm here to teach you."

Though Gavin was already pretty sure he knew the answer to this, he asked anyway.

"Teach me what?"

"Why," the man said, "to be a werewolf of course. You were bitten last night, as I'm sure you recall, and you need someone to show you the ropes. Can't have new werewolves going around terrorizing the countryside, attacking people willy-nilly, now can we?"

"Isn't that," Gavin asked, "pretty much exactly what happened to me?"

"You understand perfectly! Yes, and that particular aberrant werewolf has been dealt with most severely, I assure you."

"Is he dead?"

"She," the man said, "and no, she's not. It's harder to kill a werewolf than you might think, especially for us, as we can't handle silver without doing ourselves rather serious harm. She is, however, quite incapable of going anywhere. Incredible strength doesn't do you much good without any leverage. We strung her up a bit. For her own good, of course." He seemed quite pleased with himself.

"Shit. I can't kill myself, can I?"

"Why in the world would you want to do that?"

"I'm a werewolf now, right?"

"Yes. If there was any doubt, it was removed when your arm grew back."

"I made a promise that I'd kill myself if this ever happened to me. I don't want to be the terror of my county, or anyone else's either."

"You don't have to be, son. That's what I'm telling you. I can help you learn to live with the beast inside you and you can have a fairly normal life. Except on the full moon, when you'll need to be sequestered and you can't risk having children as you might pass on the curse."

"I can't ever get laid? Kill me now."

"New wolves are always so dramatic. Of course you can have sexual relations; you just have to take precautions so you do not create a werewolf baby. This thing is an abomination that frequently kills and eats its way out of its mother by the seventh month of pregnancy."

"Jesus."

"Quite. Always, always wear a condom; this is not optional. Now then, in a few short years, I shall have you ready to go back out in public as a sane, productive member of human society. Of course, every month you will have to return for the full moon to be restrained. Ready?"

Gavin looked at the man. He seemed to have everything pretty well under control, to pass as human. Though, to be sure, Gavin could smell Wolf on him. He could smell others, too, not far, right down the hall in fact. He breathed deeply, tried to make it look like a sigh as he investigated this new sense. Outside, he could only smell trees, flowers and grass. No wolves. He looked at his 'patron'.

"I'm sorry," he said. "I didn't catch your name."

"How rude of me. I haven't given it. I am called Gideon; I had a surname once, but I find them extraneous. And yours?"

"Gavin. Surname optional as well, I guess. Look, Gideon, I have a powerful thirst. Do you think I could get some water?"

"Of course! Gavin. An excellent name. We need more hard G's around here. I'll be right back with a trough."

As soon as Gavin could no longer hear Gideon's footsteps, though he could still smell him and the other wolves, he opened his window and looked down. Four floors to the ground. He figured his new and improved body could handle it. He pulled the screen out and jumped, his hospital gown flapping around him. It took a long time to land, and the whole time, Gavin thought he was really going to hurt himself when he hit, but he didn't. His legs, which only hours ago had been so much shredded meat, took the impact with hardly a jolt. He laughed out loud at his new strength and he ran. As far as he could tell, they never even gave chase.

***

Gavin got his bearings pretty fast, his enhanced senses laying out the land for him on an instinctive level. And, holy crap, could he run! Sometimes, his hand would drop to the ground, or a tree or rock, adding stability and speed; at one point, on rough terrain, both hands were in full use, and it was almost like running on all fours. It was exhilarating! He knew, of course, what this new strength and speed meant: it came with a price, and Gavin did not want to pay it. Deer, okay; livestock, sure, but human beings? No way, sir. Not going to happen. He headed east, toward the coast. He got there at dusk.

Catching his breath, he laid on his back; as the color bled from the world, Gavin saw the moon rise above the horizon. It was waning, having been full the night before, but it was still plenty big. It stirred something in him, something awful, something primal. He could feel his body react, begin to change. He fought it, but he lost.

***

This time, when he woke up, Gavin felt incredible; it was as if he'd dined out at a fancy restaurant, put away a few

29

shots of good scotch and had profound, life-altering sex. He was grinning like a fool. He rolled over on his side and his grin died; there was the mutilated carcass of a woman, maybe a teenage girl. It was hard to tell, as there wasn't enough left. The only reason he knew it was female at all was the one remaining breast, naked and bloody. Gavin threw up; it was violent and painful and in it he could see chunks of meat and blood and hair. He threw up again and again until he was just dry-heaving.

He pushed himself away from the corpse, scratching his bare skin on low branches. Of course, he thought, I'm naked. Because I changed. Gavin looked around him, desperate. He wanted to take it back, but since he couldn't, he fled. He ran, naked and not caring; he could smell the sea and ran toward it. It was still early, and only a few people were up and out. Those that saw him stared, but no one tried to stop him. I wouldn't either, Gavin thought; if I saw a naked man covered in blood, I would leave him the hell alone.

He got to the beach and found a boat he knew he could drive; he was a lousy sailor, but a motorboat was close enough to a car that he could handle it. He checked to make sure the engine had enough gas, and oil, and then remembering what he looked like, took a moment to wash off in the water by the dock. Gavin was cold and wet now, but it was an improvement. He still needed some clothes, but the blood was gone. Gavin unmoored the boat and fired up the engine. He left New Jersey behind, hopefully forever.

***

It had been a long time since he could see land, or another boat for that matter. It was quiet out here, peaceful. Gavin let the boat drift and took a nap.

A sudden lurch woke him up, and figured he'd maybe hit a sandbar. Gavin sat up and looked over the edge, but all he could see was water. He was hot in the afternoon sun, so he jumped in to cool off. As soon as he was underwater, he was slammed into and felt a sudden, rending pain in his right arm, and a scrape like harsh sandpaper along his ribs and hip on that side. Gavin grabbed the boat with his left hand and pulled himself up with athletic ease. His right arm was missing from the elbow down.

"What the fuck," he shouted, "is up with this arm lately? Is it yummy? Huh? Hey, shark! I'm talking to you."

The shark, a big Tiger, maybe seven, eight feet long was circling the boat a few feet below the surface. Gavin looked at his arm. The blood stopped pumping out, then stopped flowing; he watched, fascinated as the bone, muscle, veins and arteries began to regrow. He could actually see it happening, slowly at first then faster as it got closer to being whole; soon enough, his arm and hand were back, the skin quite pink and smooth, but already the hair was growing in. Gavin laughed, triumphant. He held his new arm over the water, taunting the shark.

"Is that all you got? I could do this all day!" The shark, seeing him close to the water, breached, all teeth and menace. Gavin leaned out of the way just in time and punched it in the snout, hard, with his new right hand. The shark fell back, stunned and in pain.

"I'll be damned," Gavin said. "That really works." The shark must have had enough, as it was swimming away from the boat. Gavin was annoyed.

"Uh-uh. I don't think so. You took my arm, pal. You don't get away with a little bump on the nose." Gavin triggered the change, without really knowing how, and leaped off the boat. His bellow turned into a growl as his body became a large wolf. He was trying to land on the shark, but he fell short by a few feet. The shark whipped around and slammed into him, jaws first. It pushed Gavin through the water, chewing his torso, trying to swallow him. Wolf Gavin bent himself farther than should have been possible and bit down on the shark's eye, rupturing it. It squirted like a cherry tomato in his mouth. He bit harder, fighting through the tough skin; he used his claws, both front and back to dig deep furrows in the shark. Blood was spreading out from them both in the water; other sharks were eagerly headed their way, but they were not yet close. The shark was gnawing at Wolf Gavin, cutting him in half, but not fast enough; Wolf Gavin had eaten well into the things head already and found its small, but tasty brain. Even though it was dead, the damn thing kept chewing, though it stopped swimming and started to sink. Uh oh, thought Wolf Gavin, twisting his body, trying to escape the jaws. He could smell a lot of blood, and he knew he'd have big, nasty company soon. He shifted again, and was glad for all the protein he just ate, because shifting is tiring. Human again, he used his hands to pry open the shark's jaws. He was only about ten feet down now, holding his breath. Gavin put his feet on the dead shark and shoved off, heading for air. The boat was only about forty feet away. Still bleeding, but already healing nicely, Gavin swam for the boat.

When the next shark attacked, he anticipated it and turned in the water to face it. There were others; he could sense them in the water, but they were busy eating the dead shark below. Only this one went after the live target. Lucky. As the shark hit the surface, mouth open, Gavin shoved his right arm, of course, into its mouth all the way to the throat. A shark is not capable of looking surprised, but this one tried.

"Got you," Gavin said, his face right up against the shark's nose. He flexed his arm and shot his hand upward, the jagged teeth doing terrible things to his biceps; he felt the soft, squishy stuff inside its head and he squeezed. The shark went still, and Gavin left his arm in its mouth, swimming left-handed back to the boat. When he got there, he flipped the big fish on board; this one was smaller than the Tiger, maybe five feet; he climbed up after and sat down, looking at his prize. The sun set as his wounds closed.

***

Gavin survived at sea for six days, living on shark meat and fish blood; when he finally found land, he was the thirstiest he could ever remember being, but alive and strong. It is damn hard to kill a werewolf. He landed his boat in New Hampshire, where there were lots and lots of woods. He stayed well away from population centers; one human life was more than he ever wanted to take, but he stayed near the coast. And he swam a lot; he went out to the deep water, too, because that's where the fun was; because nobody put up a fight like a shark.

KEN MACGREGOR

Killer Bagel

Carl woke up hungry. He rolled out of bed and into the shower, stale smoke and beer sweat sluicing off him and down the drain. As he dried off, the church in the next block rang the bell, as it did every hour. He counted them. Ten. He felt each one like a blow to the head.

"I am never drinking again," Carl mumbled. It was his mantra.

Carl lurched out the front door; the sunshine lancing into his brain as he hustled to put on the sunglasses. Avoiding human contact, he made his way to Max's Deli. His stomach craved bread, and his brain coffee. Thank god ten am was a slow time for Max. Early mornings and around lunchtime, it got very loud in there. Max himself was at the counter. He looked up and beamed.

"Mr. Carl!" Max always used "Mr." or "Ms." with his customers' first names. It was oddly endearing. Carl gave Max a weak smile and ordered a large coffee and an everything bagel.

"So sorry, Mr. Carl," Max said, regret clear on his face. "We had to 86 the everything bagels. Garlic and onion we still have; that's as close as it gets. I give you the coffee for free, to make up for it, okay?"

"No, no," Carl said. "Garlic is fine. I'll pay for the coffee. Things run out. It happens. Don't worry about it."

"Thank you," Max grinned. He yelled to the kitchen. "Drop a garlic! You want cream cheese and lox with that?" Carl's stomach did a backflip when it heard cream cheese, but lox would be good. He ordered it that way and sat down on the cushioned bench, sipping the too-hot coffee in the to-go cup.

"Order up!" Carl's head whipped around; he had been woolgathering, and the movement hurt him. Wincing, he got up, paid and left the deli, coffee and bagel in tow. A tiny wisp of steam rose from the sipping oval in the lid. This time, he remembered to wear his shades before he got outside.

Carl found an empty wooden bench in the park nearby. He sat down, set his cup next to him, making sure it was level and wouldn't tip over. He opened the bag, removed the bagel; the lox were wrapped separately. Carl pulled the halves of the warm, crispy bagel apart and slid the pink fish inside. He brought the food to his mouth and took a bite.

When it hit his taste buds, he was shocked. Carl had never tasted anything so good! Ravenous, he wolfed down the rest. Carl sat there, stunned for a moment. That was delicious.

Mechanically, he lifted the coffee to his lips and drank some. It was cold.

The church bells down the street rang once. One o'clock? How could that be? He had been sitting there for two-and-a-half hours. Carl shifted his weight, and realized both legs and his butt had fallen asleep. The pins and needles were excruciating. But they were nothing compared to what came next.

Carl's stomach clenched. He doubled over. It felt like a spear was in his gut, a big one. The pain migrated. It went lower. The pressure was awful and intense. Carl lifted his shirt to look at himself. Something was pushing against his abdomen. He could see it, bulging under his skin. Watching and feeling it move inside him made him puke. He lurched to the side, but a lot of it got on him.

The thing inside Carl moved again and the pain almost made him pass out. He fell to the ground, writhing, groaning. He was distantly aware of a voice nearby. A man was talking to Carl, asking him if he needed help, if he needed a doctor.

"Get it outta me!" It was all he could manage. The stranger put a hand on Carl's shoulder. His other hand pulled out a cell phone and dialed 911.

"Oh god! Oh my fucking god!" Carl ripped at his belt buckle, tore it open. He pulled his pants down as fast as he could. The bystander backpedaled, worried that this man might be crazy.

Carl bucked off the ground, screaming. Blood flecks flew out of his anus and the other man gasped and backed even further away. Carl's whole body went rigid. He screamed once more and passed out.

The other man approached Carl, morbid curiosity forcing him to look. There on the ground lay a blood-covered lump. It was round, bumpy and looked too big to have been passed by a human being. The man looked closer, leaning in.

"What the hell," he said. He recognized it. A bagel. A bagel that had been chewed and swallowed. Somehow, it had put itself back together inside this poor bastard's stomach and forced its way out. "Jesus."

Sirens approached the park, followed closely by police and an ambulance. The man told them what happened, nodding when they looked at him like he was crazy.

"I know what it sounds like," he said. "But, that's what happened. I'm not going to make something up just 'cause the truth sounds crazy."

He tried to show them the bagel, but it was gone. Of course it was.

The EMTs loaded Carl into the ambulance. Before the doors closed, the man heard one of the EMTs shout, "He's flatlining!"

The man looked at the blood on the ground. There was a lot of it. Still no sign of the bagel. He shook his head. Maybe I'm losing it, he thought.

Then, he saw it.

The bagel was sitting on the bench, next to paper cup with a plastic lid. The lumpy circle of toasted dough was still wet with blood, but there seemed to be less of it. *How did it get there? What the hell is going on?*

He took a step toward the bench, never taking his eyes off the bagel. He squatted in front of the bench, leaned in for a closer look.

The bagel moved. The man flinched, but stayed where he was. He couldn't take his eyes off the thing. It moved again, a little. The man watched, fascinated. He was pretty sure no one had ever seen anything like this. The bagel was inching its way across the bench in his direction. The whole event was surreal and captivating. The man noted that it left a trail of blood on the wood and wondered how long the bagel would take to reach the edge.

Then, Bang! It flew into his face, covering his nose and mouth. He couldn't breathe: garlic and another man's blood and feces filling his nostrils. He pried at it with his fingers, but it was already forcing itself into him, filling his throat and sinuses.

The man choked and gagged and clawed at his nose and mouth; he had time to think, *Well, this is a stupid and absurd way to die.* Then he was gone.

***

Max looked up as the bells on the door chimed. He grinned.

"Ms. Jessica!" he gave her a friendly wave. "So nice to see you."

"Thanks, Max," Jessica Saunders said. "Do you have any sesame bagels left?"

"Oh no," Max said, full of regret. "I'm so sorry. We only have garlic left."

"Okay," she said. "I'll take one of those. Toasted with lox, please."

KEN MACGREGOR

Disaster Blanket

My father taught me to always plan ahead. This has, for the most part, made my life much easier. I did well in school; I had a good job; I found a wonderful (and, it turns out, incredibly supportive) husband.

But, it was planning ahead that ultimately ruined everything.

Bill and I had our house (a fixer-upper we got for a song), our careers were both solid and we decided to have kids. Two: just enough to replace us when we're gone. I told him I didn't care, but secretly I wanted two girls. Still, I made the blanket yellow, just in case.

I started it when I was visiting Granny Bea. It was her 87th birthday, but she didn't want a party; just a few family members and the two friends she had left. Granny Bea had been an avid knitter, but her hands no longer worked right. I asked her if I could use her needles and some yellow yarn.

Everyone else had left, but we had a long drive, so Bill was napping. I had finished a few rows when Granny Bea asked what I was making.

"A baby blanket," I said. She beamed at me and said she had no idea and how wonderful.

"No, Granny. I'm not pregnant. Just planning ahead." She frowned at me.

"Child," she said, "don't you know it's bad luck?" I scoffed and went back to knitting.

"I don't think you understand, Jennifer; you never, ever make something for a baby you haven't conceived. Nothing good can come from it, child. And plenty bad."

"Granny, I know you are pretty old-school, but this is the twenty-first century. I just don't believe in superstitions. No offense, of course. You believe whatever you want, but once I get pregnant, I'm afraid I'll have too many other things to do, so I'm doing this now."

Granny Bea had very little to say after that. When we left, she gave me a dry kiss on the cheek, looked at me for a long moment and shook her head sadly.

In the car, Bill asked what was wrong, but I blew it off. Just Granny Bea being superstitious, I told him. Don't worry about it, I said. I would eat those words.

I finished the blanket months later; it was lovely and soft, bright and cozy. Almost immediately, I got pregnant.

Everything was textbook: oh, I had some nausea, but never morning sickness; I developed a strong aversion to the smell of cheddar cheese, which made me sad. Otherwise, I was healthy, happy and glowing. At the second ultrasound, the one where they determine gender (we both wanted to be surprised), we had our first inkling that something was wrong. The doctor made a small noise in her throat, unconsciously, I think. Bill and I looked at her. We couldn't see the screen.

"Oh," she said, smiling. "It's nothing. Just a slightly unusual phenomenon: during fetal growth, there is a tiny, vestigial tail; it's perfectly normal, and we all have it. However, by this stage it's usually gone, and your child still has one. It's rare, but hardly cause for alarm." In my mind's eye, Granny Bea is frowning at me and shaking her head.

"A tail?" Bill laughed. "Cool." I hit him gently. The doctor assured us that other than this tiny, unexpected-but-perfectly-harmless detail, the child appeared to be healthy: ten fingers and toes and everything was coming along nicely.

My breasts and belly grew to truly alarming proportions and simple things like standing up from a chair had become Olympic level events. I watched a tiny, perfectly formed footprint glide from one side of me to the other, under my skin. I was filled with anticipation and love, yet I couldn't get that dinner scene from "Alien" out of my head. Eventually, the baby 'dropped'. This is the term they use when the mother stops carrying high and the child is almost ready to come out. But, it's so appropriate; my whole middle went 'thunk' down below. Well, not really, but it sure looked like it. This meant I was due any day now. I'd been dreaming of meeting my baby for a few weeks; sometimes it was a girl, sometimes a boy. I was finally going to know.

I think Bill was even more excited than I was.

Nine days later, my water broke; I was at the dry cleaners. They were very sweet about it. Called me a cab and everything. I called Bill on the way, and he met me at the hospital mere minutes after I arrived. He was not quite panicking. It was cute.

I'm a little fuzzy on the details of labor. I know it was awful, but I think I blocked a lot of it out. I've done that a lot since then, too. The one thing I can still remember vividly is after the final push, the final moment of pressure and pain, despite the drugs, is that moment of silence when my child came out of me. I couldn't see, of course, but Bill could. His mouth was hanging open, his eyes wide.

"What is it?" I was starting to panic. "What's wrong with my baby? Why is it so quiet?" I tried to sit up, which was a mistake. Bill and a nurse took a shoulder each and eased me back down. They made soothing noises. I wasn't fooled.

"Bill," I looked at my husband. "What's wrong, honey? Why is everyone quiet? Why is the baby quiet?"

"Jenny, honey, it's okay. The baby's breathing. He's alive..."

"He? It's a boy?" Bill paused, too long.

"Yes," he hedged. "It's a boy. But..." He looked at the doctor, who was cleaning off my baby; I knew this because of where he was and the way he was moving, but he was between me and the child, so I couldn't see. The doctor turned, his face professionally blank, and brought a small bundle wrapped in a blanket to me. Bill moved a little away so I could take my son. He was tiny, so light. The blanket partly obscured his face so only one eye was visible and it was closed. Just this tiny part of my child's face filled my heart with pride and love. Gently, I moved the blanket off his face so I could see my son.

He was... wrong.

Bill was, I think, holding his breath as I removed the rest of the blanket. I think maybe I was, too. The lower half of my boy's face protruded, snout-like. His nose was two slits. I supported his head and looked at the rest. His arms seemed normal, but his hands were skeletal things, fingers too long, tapering to points. His legs bent backward at the knee, like a cat, or dog, or goat, or something. His ten toes grew together, connected by tough-looking skin, pawlike. I could see tiny white claws curving just below the surface. I could feel something odd on his back, so I turned him over. There was the tail, of course, almost as long as he was tall; I pretty much expected that at this point. The wings, though, came as a shock.

Nobody spoke. I turned my baby boy back around and looked at his face. Inhuman, but not ugly. Sort of feline really.

44

He opened his tiny eyes and looked at me. I grinned at him and his green eyes sparkled at me.

"I want to call him Benjamin," I said to Bill. "It was his grandfather's name."

"Honey," Bill said carefully. "Are you okay?"

"Oh, Bill," I said, "I know he's different, but he's our son. How could we not love him?"

Benjamin only took a couple of years to show us exactly how. The media circus died down after a year or so, but once they left us alone, Ben started acting out. He was bigger than other kids his age, three-year-old-size at one. And strong. For a while, it was just tantrums and screaming. Every day. That's hard to take. But, that's parenting, right? You take the good with the bad. You develop a thick skin after a while.

Then, when Benjamin was almost two, he ate the cat.

Of course, that was unacceptable and he had to be punished. I hated to do it, but it was for his own good. His third birthday party was a small affair. Just the three of us. We put three small candles in a raw flank steak and tossed it to him. The heavy chain slithered across the floor as Benjamin moved to get his 'cake'. We didn't light the candles, of course. We were worried he'd get burned. He's just a child, you know? Bill and I sang Happy Birthday, only a little off-key.

"I love you," I said. He looked up at me, bright green eyes reflecting the hall light. Blood from the steak dripped off his snout. He reached behind him and brought out an old, tattered yellow blanket. A blanket I made. He held it to his cheek.

"Momma," he slurred. "I love you. Let me go." I cried, and told him I can't. I hated this, but two kids disappeared in our neighborhood. Their bones are at the bottom of the lake seven miles from here, but we can't keep this up. We're not monsters.

Well, Bill and I aren't.

Bad Squirrel

"Damn it! Squirrel's on the birdfeeder again!" Grampa was turning red. "I greased the damn pole, put on that metal high-hat thingie and cut away all the branches within thirty feet! How the hell is that little Tree Rat getting on there?"

I knew better than to interrupt. Grampa said he was gonna kill the damn thing this time. I went back to my book.

After a moment, I heard the front door bang open. This was new. I went to the window to watch. Grampa was walking around the house, wearing a light jacket and carrying a rifle. He looked calm, almost serene. He stopped at the corner of the house and looked at the feeder. The squirrel looked up from its meal and gazed back at Grampa. Time held its breath. Grampa raised the rifle to his shoulder. The squirrel twitched its tail once, twice. Grampa released his breath and squeezed the trigger. The birdhouse exploded, seeds pouring onto the ground in a torrent. The squirrel was torn nearly in half. It lay amongst the seeds, its tiny, hand-like paws scrabbling for purchase.

"Gotcha," Grampa said. "Gotcha."

***

Grampa bought a new feeder and hung it in the same spot. He installed all the old precautions and some new ones. The birds began to come back. Grampa was happy again. Then...

47

"Damn it!" A squirrel was on the feeder, somehow slipping past the defenses. Grampa stormed outside and yelled at it. The squirrel looked at him, then slowly turned and walked around the feeder. When its side was to us, me watching from the window, we knew it was the same one. Two halves, barely held together with strips of furry skin.

Impossible. Awful. Grampa stared, his mind unable to accept what his eyes saw. The squirrel made a full circuit of the feeder and looked my Grampa in the eye.

It leaped.

Grampa jerked back in terror as the squirrel came at him. He fell. He hit his head on a paving stone.

The ER docs tried to save him, but they said his heart couldn't handle the trauma. Said it was 'overstressed' by the injury. They said 'cardiac arrest brought on by a traumatic brain injury', but I knew better. It was the squirrel.

***

These days, not too many birds use the feeder; sometimes a crow will come, unkempt things missing an eye or a foot. They never stay long. But we keep it well-stocked. Because my children are starting to have children now. We keep the feeder stocked, I will tell them, because the squirrel is there every day, and probably always will be.

It's part of our lives now, though we may hate it. We will continue to do it. There are only four of us left (soon to be five), and we're survivors. We know how to live. We keep the feeder stocked. Keep the squirrel happy. And, for god's sake, don't make it angry.

PROTÉGÉ

Jefferson Elementary School sat quiet in the afternoon sun; birds chirped in the nearby park and traffic ambled by at a relaxed pace.

Without warning, the double doors burst open, spewing forth a sea of miniature humanity, shrieking with the twin joys of freedom and being young.

Diesel engines rumbled to life and kids got on buses, jostling for their favorite seats.

Simon waited until his best friend was almost on the bus, gave Nick a high five and said he'll see him tomorrow. Simon walked away from the slowly thinning horde and headed home. Along the way, he kicked small rocks and walked atop low, stone walls, acting out superhero fantasies. Finally, he got to the unlocked door and let himself in.

"Mom!"

"In the kitchen!" she shouted back. Simon dropped his backpack on the floor by the couch, forgetting about it instantly. He walked into the kitchen and hugged his mom, who raised her elbows out of the way. She was washing dishes and her hands were covered in soapy water. She smiled at him and he smiled back.

"How was school?"

"Bo-ring" He rolled his eyes.

"Again?" his mom asked in mock dismay.

"I know, right?" Simon said. "I keep waiting for it to be a Carnival of Awesome, but I am always disappointed."

Harmony laughed. It made him smile.

"And, how was your day, Mom?"

"It was nice actually," she said. "I got to spend an hour in the hammock reading Vonnegut."

"Bo-ring!"

"Why don't you go change, so you can go outside and get filthy?" Simon bolted for the stairs. She yelled after him, "I'll call you when dinner's ready!"

***

The next morning, while Simon was in school, his mom went shopping. She was carrying a hand basket, only getting what she needed for the next couple days. She exchanged brief pleasantries with a mom she sort-of knew. The cashier was young, maybe sixteen, struggling with acne, but polite and genuine; Harmony wished him a lovely day, too.

On her way out, a flyer on the community bulletin board caught her eye. It was crimson paper, thick, handwritten with a calligraphy pen or brush. It was very ornate and pretty and said: 'Classical Piano Lessons. All Skill Levels. Very Reasonably Priced.' There were tear-away tabs cut into the bottom with a phone number, also done by hand.

Harmony was enchanted by the idea of Simon learning piano and took down the whole poster. She put it in her purse and looked around, guilty, half expecting someone to scold her.

***

That night, just after dinner, before Simon cleared the plates, his job, he drained half the milk in his glass all at once.

"Aaaaahhhh..." he said, wiping his mouth with the back of his hand dramatically. "Best. Milk. Ever."

"Glad you like it," Harmony said. "Can I ask you a question, Simon?"

"You just did. But, I'm feeling generous. Go ahead and ask me another one."

"Kind of you, sir," she smiled. "Would you like to learn to play piano?"

"I don't know. I never thought about it. Why?"

Harmony reached over to a side table and grabbed her purse. She pulled out the red flyer and handed it to him. He read it over and looked up at her.

"It's really pretty handwriting."

"Yeah."

"I don't know, mom," Simon hedged. "You remember when I tried to learn trombone?"

"Simon, you were six. You could barely lift the thing. A piano is much less... awkward."

Simon looked at the flyer again. He ran his fingers over the letters. He set it down and assumed a very serious, concentrating face. He arched an eyebrow, lifted his hands and 'played' piano very dramatically on the table. Harmony laughed and he joined her.

"Okay. I'll give it a shot," he said. "But if I hate it after a month, can I quit?"

"Two months."

"Deal." Simon nodded and they shook on it.

***

The following Saturday, around 11 am, Harmony and Simon found themselves in a nondescript, suburban home.

They sat side-by-side on a worn loveseat in a small sitting room. The walls were adorned with framed prints: there were photos and paintings of grand pianos. After a moment, an interior door opened and a tall, gaunt, older man appeared and looked at them for several seconds in silence. He had unusually long fingers. Harmony and Simon were uncomfortable, but afraid to be rude. Finally, Simon couldn't take it anymore.

"Hi," he said standing up. "I'm Simon and I'd like to learn to play the piano."

"Well," replied the man. He had a mild, German accent. "By an odd coincidence, I happen to teach that particular instrument." He smiled at Simon and Harmony, but it was unnatural, as if his mouth didn't quite know how.

"That works out well then," said Harmony. "Doesn't it?"

"Yes. Forgive my rudeness," he said "I am Klaus Engel. Does the boy have any musical training?"

"He tried to take up the trombone a couple years ago, but it didn't go very well."

"I kept dropping it," said Simon. "And tripping over the slide."

"Please do not drop my piano."

Harmony and Simon stared at him. He laughed, a wheezing, coughing sound.

"It is a joke." They laughed politely and he suddenly serious again. "Please, come and meet the instrument. Perhaps you will be friends."

They all went through the door from which Klaus first entered. It led to a small, somewhat plain room that was dominated by a beautiful, shining black grand piano on a dais, the top open to reveal the insides. Beyond the piano, one wall was all windows looking out onto a wilderness of trees. The overall effect was breathtaking.

"Wow," breathed Simon.

"What a gorgeous piano," Harmony said at the same time.

"You are kind to say so," said Klaus.

Simon approached the piano, almost reverently. He looked at Klaus. "May I?"

Klaus nodded, watching him. Simon sat on the bench and opened the cover over the keyboard. He looked at the keys, white and black, long and short. He passed his hand over the keys without touching them, and then rested his fingers very lightly on the surface of the keys. Harmony was bemused; Klaus was watching intently.

"They're cold."

"Yes."

"It's so pretty, Mom." Simon was hooked. "I want to learn how to play."

"Well, honey. That's why we're here."

"I know," he says. "But, before I was just humoring you. Now, I really want to."

"Miss," Klaus began, "I'm sorry. I didn't catch your name."

"Harmony."

"Ah," Klaus said, grimacing his non-smile. "The child comes from music. It is auspicious. Harmony, it has been my experience that no one learns well while their mother is in the room, but I will understand if you wish to stay for this first lesson."

"I'd like that," Harmony said. "Simon is very responsible. I'm sure he'll be fine without me in the future."

"Good," said Klaus, turning to Simon. "Touch the keys again. Feel the weight of them under your fingertips. Start at the far left end of the keyboard and play each note. Gently, gently, boy. This is not a drum. You do not bludgeon; you caress. Better. Work your way along. Listen to each note. Feel each key. Is there resistance? Can you feel the hammers inside as they strike the wires? Good. Now, go back the other way, and feel all the notes again."

Simon was intent. He caressed the keys as instructed. He listened to each note. He did feel the hammers striking the wires. He was fascinated by the cause and effect of his fingers touching the keys and clear, loud notes coming from inside the piano. When he reached the left end of the keyboard again, he smiled at Klaus. Klaus nodded his head. He turned to Harmony.

"I will teach this boy."

***

The next morning, while Simon was in school, Harmony 'Googled' Klaus Engel, telling herself it was idle curiosity; certainly, she was not worried about leaving Simon alone with him. He was an odd old man, to be sure, but her son knew when to leave if he had to. And, he did take two years of Judo. Still, she was a mother, so she checked up on him.

In his late teens and early twenties, Klaus had been a world class pianist, the toast of Germany, a *wunderkind*. But, crippling arthritis in his mid-thirties ended his playing career and he disappeared into obscurity.

There was a video link on the page and Harmony clicked on it. Even through her mediocre laptop speakers, she could tell it was beautiful. The piece was twelve minutes long, something by Beethoven that she recognized, but couldn't name. This was unlike anything else she'd ever heard. This was raw, visceral playing. This was what music should sound like. And Simon's going to learn from this man? My god, he'll be brilliant! The music stopped and Klaus bowed formally to the audience, who stood and offered thunderous applause. Harmony closed her laptop and stared at it.

"Wow."

**

After school, Simon stopped home, wolfed down a PB&J sandwich and jumped on his bike. Harmony kissed him just below the helmet, accidentally getting part of his ear. He shook his head a little, grinned at her and took off.

**

Simon was practicing his scales; Klaus called out notes, and Simon played them. After a while, Simon stopped and looked at his teacher.

"What?"

"How come you don't play anymore?"

"I played for years. Now it is your turn."

"Mom said you were really great," Simon said, "back in the day."

"Your mother is checking up on me?"

"Wouldn't you? If it was your kid, I mean?"

"Of course," Klaus said. "I am not offended, just asking."

"So," Simon persisted. "Why'd you quit? Playing, I mean."

"My hands," Klaus said, looking at them. "They hurt when I play for more than a few minutes. It is arthritis... a curse."

"So," Simon said, "You could play for a few minutes without pain?"

"Yes. Why?"

"I'd like to hear it." Klaus looked at him for several seconds, considering.

"Move over," he said. Simon did, and Klaus sat next to him on the bench. He closed his eyes and put his hands on the keys. What came out of that instrument was sad and beautiful, unearthly and profound. Simon was blown away.

"That," he said, "is the prettiest thing I've ever heard. How did you learn to play like that?"

"I sold my soul to the devil," Klaus said. Simon rolled his eyes.

"If I sold my soul to the devil," he said. "I'd get something really cool for it."

"Oh? Such as?"

"Immortality," said Simon, very smug. "That way, the Devil would never get to collect, and I'd have all the time in the world to learn piano or anything else I want."

"Very smart," said Klaus. "I wish I'd thought of that."

***

A few weeks passed; Harmony and Simon were in the back yard. At the edge of the yard was an old swing set from Simon's early childhood that was starting to rust. Harmony was weeding her flower garden; Simon was throwing a ball up in the air and catching it again and again.

"So," Simon said.

"So," his mom returned.

"Klaus says I'm getting really good."

"You call him Klaus?"

"Sure," Simon said. "He's cool like that. He says maybe someday I could be really great at piano. Says I have a 'gift'."

"That's great, Simon! I always thought you were talented, but, you know, I'm a little biased... But if your piano teacher thinks so, too... wow. And he was incredible in his prime, so, I guess he'd know."

"Okay, Mom," Simon said with a back-up-a-little gesture. "Let's not get all carried away. Klaus said maybe, and I could be... I still have a lot of work to do. I just started learning, you know?"

"Of course," Harmony said. "Rome not being built in a day and all that... it's still cool, though."

"Yeah," Simon smiled at her. "It is."

***

Back in the room with all the windows, Klaus was listening to Simon play. It was a fairly simple piece, but Simon played it well. He finished with a flourish that was not on the sheet music. Klaus's eyebrows shot up.

"What was that?" he demanded.

"I don't know," Simon shrugged. "It just seemed to need something else at the end."

"You are improvising."

"Is that okay?"

"It is," Klaus paused, searching for the word. "Unusual."

"Why?"

57

"Well, Simon," Klaus said, "you have not been playing long enough to be improvising."

"Sorry."

"You misunderstand me, Simon. It is a skill that should only come with years of training and performing, not months. You are making intuitive leaps that are, quite frankly, astounding."

"I am?" Simon asked. "Cool." Klaus looked at him.

"You want to cultivate this gift, do you?"

"Sure," Simon said. "I mean, that's why we're here, right?"

"Indeed it is."

"All right then," Klaus smiled. "Let's get back to it, shall we? This time, if you feel like improvising at any point in the piece, go ahead and do it. We'll see how it goes."

***

Harmony was cutting small slits into the skin of a whole chicken and sliding garlic slivers underneath. She learned this trick from her own mother. The garlic infuses the whole bird and tastes amazing. Simon was doing his homework, but was tapping his foot to music in his head, and would put down the pencil to tap out 'notes' on the table. Harmony watched him.

"Dinner in about 40 minutes, kiddo."

"Mm-hm." Simon said. Harmony watched his hands.

"Whatcha doin'?" Simon looked up.

"Math homework."

"To me," Harmony said, "It looks like you're playing piano."

"Oh yeah" Simon said. "That, too. Helps me think."

"Well, whatever gets the job done, right?" But, Simon was no longer listening. He tapped fingers and toes to the music in his head. Harmony watched him for a few more seconds. She was filled with a sudden sense of love and pride for her son. Then she remembered the chicken and put it in the oven.

***

At Klaus's piano, Simon was playing a complex piece of music and doing it well. He stopped when he mis-keyed a note.

"Damn," Simon said, unconsciously mimicking his mother when she's annoyed.

"Start from the beginning, please."

Simon was frustrated.

"I know this piece. That shouldn't have happened."

"Simon," Klaus's voice was calm, soothing. "You are too hard on yourself. Six months ago, you had never touched a piano. Now, you are playing something it takes most students three years to even attempt. You are a wunderkind. Start from the beginning."

Simon started to play again. He closed his eyes as he played, rocking slightly. Klaus watched Simon's face and listened to the music pouring from the piano. Simon finished the piece. It was flawless. He dropped his head and sat in silence. Klaus slowly applauded and Simon's head snapped up. He was grinning.

"Nailed it, didn't I?"

"Yes, you did." Klaus gave Simon his awful smile.

***

Harmony and Simon were watching the BBC series 'Planet Earth,' eating popcorn and silently marveling at the cinematography.

"I've been thinking," Simon said.

"Yeah?" Harmony said. "What's up?"

"The school has a talent show they do every year."

"And?"

"I think," Simon said, "I want to play piano for it."

"You really think you're ready?" Harmony caught herself: "For an audience, I mean."

"Sure." Simon was confident. "Klaus started performing when he was eight. Mozart was only six." Harmony's eyebrows climbed up.

"Mozart?"

"Yeah. Of course, he was insanely brilliant. But, I'm good, Mom. I really am. And I'm ready to play for a crowd. Especially since it's just grade school kids and their parents. Nobody's expectations are going to be too high."

"That's true," she said. "Okay, honey. I'll talk to your teacher about it."

Simon leaned over the bowl to kiss his Mom on the cheek.

"Thanks, Mom. You're the best."

***

Simon stood behind the piano bench. He hesitated.

"Are you going to play?" Klaus eyed him.

"Yeah," Simon said. "One thing: I am booked as one of the acts for my school talent show in two months."

"What will you be doing?" Klaus asked.

60

"Playing piano," Simon said. "Duh."

"Interesting. Who made this decision?"

"I did."

"Good," Klaus nodded. "Sit. We must make sure you are ready."

***

The next few weeks passed in a blur of practicing and comments from Klaus: "Too fast. It is not a race. You will get to the end in good time... that's it. Let the music set the pace. Good. Good." The leaves outside the piano room windows changed from green to red and gold. One fall day, Simon finished a beautiful piece by Brahms, precise and soulful. As the last notes echoed around the room, Simon looked at his mentor. Klaus nodded.

"You are ready."

***

The grade-school auditorium was actually pretty nice; it had good acoustics enhanced by hanging microphones. The act before Simon's was a short, original comedy by some fourth and fifth graders; Simon's friend Nick is one of them, and he did most of the writing. It was pretty funny. Simon was glad for them. After the applause died down, his principal, Ms. Calloway introduced him. The grand piano was already set up just left of center stage; it was not in the same class as the one Klaus owned, but it would serve.

Simon entered from the wings wearing a small tuxedo, the sight of which elicited some titters from the audience. Simon walked to just behind the bench, turned to the audience and took a small, formal bow as he had seen pianists do in movies. He then sat at the piano, shot his cuffs and placed his hands over the keys. He waited for the sound in the audience to die down. When it did, he began to play. He played Tchaikovsky's Sixth Symphony; it is a dark and powerful piece, emotionally stirring and somewhat disturbing. Simon played it brilliantly: he was technically perfect and he invested the music with an emotional intensity that was astounding.

When he finished, there was silence as the audience realized they have witnessed something great. Then, the applause was thunderous. They rose to their feet, clapping even harder. Simon lifted his head, stood and turned toward the audience. He took a formal bow, then stood up again with a huge grin on his face. He pumped his fist in the air.

"Booyah!" He shouted and he thought he could hear his mom laugh. He walked to the wings and Samantha Knox stood there, holding juggling pins, staring at him.

"I," she said, "have to follow *that*?"

"Sorry," Simon said, shrugging and grinning. Klaus and Harmony were backstage already. His mom gave him a huge hug and told him how proud she was. Simon thanked her and looked to Klaus.

"Well?" he asked.

"Very nice," Klaus said. "Perhaps a little showboating at the end."

"Really," Simon was surprised. "I thought I played it perfectly."

"I was referring to the 'booyah'."

"Oh, yeah," Simon said. "Well, I was pretty stoked."

"Yes. Well, you should be. You, as you are so fond of saying, nailed it."

"Thanks, Klaus. And thanks for coming, too."

"Simon," Klaus said, "Hell's Legions couldn't have kept me away."

"Klaus," Simon said, "you're a little creepy sometimes."

"I will work on that."

"Who wants ice cream?" Harmony jumped in. "I'm buying."

"I don't wish to intrude..." Klaus started to leave.

"Nonsense," Harmony said. "If it weren't for you, we wouldn't have anything to celebrate. I insist."

"Then, I have no choice but to accompany you for ice cream."

"That's right," Simon said. "You don't. Come on. I'll introduce you to the awesomeness of Superman flavor."

"I am quite familiar with Superman flavor," Klaus said. "Though I find Pistachio infinitely more satisfying."

"You eat ice cream?"

"Certainly, Simon," Klaus said. "I'm not a complete barbarian."

***

Simon walked into the piano room; there was quite a lot of snow on the trees outside the windows. He walked toward the piano, but Klaus stopped him.

"Wait," he said. "Let us talk a little."

"Sure," Simon said. "What's up?"

Klaus removed a small key from his pocket and opened the drawer in a table by the window. From inside, he removed a leather-bound folder, plain, black. He reached back in and pulled out a fountain pen with an extremely sharp tip. He handed the folder to Simon; inside was a contract. Simon read it. Some of it was lawyer-ese, but he got the drift. One can become the finest piano player of his generation, for the low, low cost of one human soul.

On the signature line was 'Simon Chase'.

***

Harmony was on the couch reading a novel. She jerked upright, suddenly certain her son was in danger. The book hit the floor.

"Simon!"

***

"A long time ago," Klaus said, in almost a whisper, "you asked me how I learned to play piano like that. You remember?"

"Sure," Simon said. "You said that you sold your soul to the Devil."

"It was not joke."

"I don't understand."

"When you came to me, I thought, 'here is a child with talent. With an innate gift. I can teach this child, make him an excellent pianist. Then, maybe the Devil will take his soul instead of mine.' I thought if I could pass on my gift, I could pass on my curse. I never thought it would work of course, but the Devil liked the idea. He was quite enthusiastic about it. But, then I got to know you, Simon. In the last several months, I have come to be very fond of you, and I find that I cannot offer you up in this way."

"I don't know what to say."

"I think," Klaus said, "maybe you knew all along." They were silent for a moment.

"I am ashamed," Klaus continued, "for even thinking of sacrificing you. I am appalled at my selfishness. For my own piece of mind, I need to be honest with you."

"But you changed your mind," Simon said. "That's what counts, right?"

"It certainly makes it easier to live with myself."

Simon looked at the contract in his hands. He looked Klaus in the eye for a long moment.

"What if I were to agree to it?"

***

Harmony slammed her car into gear, and left tire tracks on the cement backing out of her driveway. She nearly collided with the Post Office truck.

***

"No," Klaus said. "You do not know what you are offering."

"Give me some credit, Klaus. I'm a smart kid. I know what I'm doing. And I think I'll be able to figure out a way out of it, too. Even if it means passing it on to some other kid when I'm old."

"It is very touching," Klaus said, "that you would even consider it, but I cannot allow it."

"Klaus, my Dad died when I was four. I barely remember him now, but I know he loved me. I couldn't stop my Dad from dying, but I can stop you from going to Hell. I've made up my mind."

"Simon," Klaus deliberated, "That is selfless and beautiful. But, I still can't let you do this. You are too young to make this decision. Did you know, for example that you would have to sign the contract in your own blood? Very painful."

65

"If the Devil were here right now, I'd sign this contract," Simon said. "And then you could get on with your life, without worrying about what happens after." Simon looked into Klaus's eyes. Klaus looked back at the boy for several seconds. Simon returned his gaze unflinching.

"Give me the pen."

***

Harmony parked the car in Klaus's driveway, throwing it into park and getting out in one motion. She left her door open and ran to the house, the keys still in the ignition and the small alarm dinging away. The front door was locked, and she beat on it with her fists.

***

"Someone's at the door," Simon said.

"I am expecting a delivery," Klaus said. "I will let them in shortly."

Simon took the pen from Klaus. He held it over his left hand for a moment, then stabbed the point into his palm. He winced and withdrew the tip. There was blood on it. He signed his name on the line of the contract. The lights dimmed to half. Simon turned to Klaus, who grinned his awful grin. Klaus snatched the contract from Simon, opened his mouth to speak, and Simon saw four distinct rows of sharp teeth, like a shark's mouth.

"Thank you very much, Simon Chance," Klaus said. "A pleasure doing business with you, my boy." His voice was horribly distorted by those teeth, but the words echoed in Simon's head, too; they were perfectly clear.

***

Forty feet away, Harmony slid down the door to lie in a heap on the front stoop, weeping for her lost son.

Zombie Ate My Girlfriend

Okay. So, I'm pathetic. Fine. I won't argue; I think so, too. But, hey! On the bright side, I'm still alive.

Of course, living with myself just got a lot harder.

Let me back up a little. Everything was great for a while there. Well, relatively great anyway. Can't really say anything's been more than 'tolerable' for the past eight months or so. But, all things considered, I was doing all right. It helped that I'd gotten very good at shooting the damn things in the head. Had to. Anywhere else and they just keep coming. I still blame George Romero. Oh, sure, he didn't invent the virus that turned half of the country into the walking dead, but he gave whoever *did* the idea. Yep. His fault, all right. Dick.

Anyway, I was doing okay. Keeping my head above water. Above ground. Hiding, mostly. Shooting when I had to. Running away a lot. It got to be pretty routine after a while. You know? It's amazing what you can get used to. Then, total fluke, I met Rebecca. First of all, she was alive, a big plus in my book. Also, she was really cute. That didn't hurt at all. Third, I totally saved her life, making me the Hero. Finally, it wasn't like either of us had a lot of dating options. We hooked up. Let me tell you something: post-apocalyptic sex is awesome.

Turns out Rebecca is a pretty good shot, too; she doesn't always get the head shot on the first try, but she always does by the second. Did. I mean 'did'. And 'was'. Fuck.

So, there we were: a couple of hardened Zombie Apocalypse veterans, fighting for our lives and trying to make a baby every chance we get. Pretty storybook, huh? It was... until it wasn't.

We were holed up (I hate that expression; why do I even use it?) in an apartment building, upper floor - sixth maybe - and were well-fed and rested, two things you really learn to appreciate. We knew we had enough food to last us maybe a week, and it seemed like a safe spot, so we let our guard down.

You can't do that. Not anymore.

The family of five, Dad, Mom, Teen Boy and Girl (Twins? So hard to tell when they're dead) and Zombie Toddler burst in through the door on day two. They were pretty far gone, so they must not have eaten for a long time. They might have been stuck in this building for weeks, maybe months. Who knows? One thing's for sure: they were very anxious to come in.

My rifle, never far from my hand, took out two of them as they crossed the threshold. Rebecca got one a second later, but that left two. Teen Girl Zombie (sounds like a Roger Corman film, doesn't it?) lunged at me, hunger making her faster than they usually are. I got the shot off at the last second, and she landed on top of me, unmoving, unbiting, half her head missing. I threw her off, disgusted by the smell and the weight of her. Rebecca was looking at me, afraid I'd been turned.

"She didn't get me," I started to say, but stopped. We had both forgotten about Zombie Toddler. The little bastard bit her on the inner thigh. Femoral blood geysered out and

Rebecca smashed her rifle butt into his tiny head, killing (if that's even the right term) the kid instantly. But, the damage was done. We might stop the bleeding, put some stitches in the wound, but no way was she going to survive. Not as a human anyway. She looked at me, pleading, asking me with her eyes to do the unthinkable. To shoot my girlfriend in the head. I wanted to, I really did. But I just couldn't do it. Pathetic, right? As I ran down the stairs, alone, I heard the shot. Turns out Rebecca had bigger balls than I.

I know, I know. I even kind of make myself a little sick. But, hey... still alive. Counts for a lot.

KEN MACGREGOR

Havin' a Bad Day

Fucker bit me. Barely broke the skin, but still! I showed him, though, didn't I? Beat his fuckin' head in. Started with the teeth, too. Poetic. Fuckin'. Justice.

That was the first time I've ever used my chucks, too. Damn fine weapon. Easily concealed, fast as hell and they do an excellent job of smashing fuckin' heads. Mine are special: got them in Chinatown. They're made from tire rubber with a lead core. Bone-breakers. I spend a couple hours a week watching Bruce Lee movies and practicing with them. I'll never be that good, but I guess I'm good enough.

My arm hurts. It itches, kind of burning feeling. Fucker probably had rabies. Or AIDS. Shit. Better not have AIDS. Nothing worse than AIDS. He did look pretty sick though... and crazy, too. I think he was crazy. Can you catch crazy? Jesus, I hope not. I may not have much in this shitty world, but I damn sure know what's real and what's not. When I used to do acid - a lot - there was always this moment, right before peaking, where I was not sure if I was going to come back. I lost my mind for just a few seconds. I had to stop doing acid. I fuckin' hated that feeling.

You can't catch crazy. I know you can't. But, looking at my arm, I'm pretty sure I caught something. Little red lines are slowly crawling up my arm away from the bite; they're following my veins. Or arteries. I don't really know the difference. One takes blood one way, and one the other, I think. Pretty much the only thing I remember from biology was Suzie Massey; she sat just behind me, one row over and always wore tiny skirts and sometimes she 'forgot' to wear underwear. So, I missed a lot of what the teacher said. Spent a lot of my free time pulling one off to her, too. Still do sometimes.

I'm getting off-topic. Hungry, too. Jesus, I'm suddenly starving. And hot. Fuck! It's hot in here. I'm going out. Maybe go to the free clinic and have a doctor look at this bite. Get some food on the way. Hamburger, maybe. No. That's not quite right. I'm craving something. Steak? Fish? Definitely something with protein.

Shit. My whole fuckin' arm is all itchy/burny now. I think I am severely allergic to that guy's spit. Okay. Food and then doctor. It's a plan. Man, I feel like shit. I'm up, I'm up. I'm going. I'm gonna puke.

Air feels good. I got this. I'm okay. It's what? Three blocks to the clinic? Yeah. And there's a Subway on the way. I'll get a meatball (still not quite right) sub and eat it on the way. Look. There's the yellow awning already. No problem. One foot in front of the other. I'm a little dizzy. It's getting hard to pick up my feet; I seem to be shuffling.

Doesn't matter. As long I get there. I eat. I see the doc. I'll be fine. Whoa. The girl at the counter looks just like Suzie Massey! Wait. No. Not really. Maybe a little. She is cute though. She asks if she can help me, but I barely hear her. My stomach growls loudly and I can't take my eyes off the pulse in her throat. Look at that thing. Bump, bump, bump against the skin. She asks if I'm okay, sounds nervous. I try to tell her I'm fine, but nothing comes out except a kind of groan. I can't seem to talk right. I take a step closer to her; she edges a little further behind the counter. I reach for her, trying to reassure her. I try to say, it's okay, Suzie, I'm just really hungry. She jerks back, into a large fridge with a glass door full of bread.

I try to calm her down, because she's screaming, and really, all I want is something to eat. It's too loud, that scream. I can't think with all that noise. I lean in and grab her pulse in my teeth. I bite down and hot, sweet liquid pours into my mouth and down my throat. I drink, so thirsty, but it's not enough. I clench my jaws together and come away with the most wonderful mouthful I've ever had.

Yes. This is it. This is what I needed. I eat my fill, every bite: so, so good. I stand there for a moment, over my meal, satisfied. But, something is nagging me. Something I need to do.

Oh yeah... the doctor's office. Maybe there will be other things to eat on the way.

THE WORLD'S STRONGEST MAN

"You know what drives me nuts, Jacob? I'll tell you, shall I? The English language drives me nuts."

Jacob nodded. He had nothing to add; he never did.

"English is so messed up," Henry continued. "For example, 'palindrome' means a word that is the same when spelled backward, but 'palindrome' backward is 'emordnilap'. I had to practice that, by the way. It should be the same both ways, don't you think?"

Jacob shrugged.

"It should. And another thing: 'lisp'. Here's a word that the people afflicted with it can't even say. That's cruel, that is."

Jacob nodded. That was true.

"And the people who have 'dyslexia' have no hope of spelling it right, you know? It's like they do it on purpose. It's messed up."

Henry and Jacob sat in silence for a bit. Jacob always did; he had no choice. The same genetic quirk that made him almost eight feet tall and as strong as any five men also rendered him mute. His throat was formed wrong: no vocal cords and a narrow esophagus. He could only eat soft foods: eggs; yogurt; protein shakes, which was okay, because those were the things he liked.

"Well," Henry said, standing. "Gotta get ready. We go up in less than an hour. Nice talking to you as always, Jacob."

Jacob nodded. He knew Henry was being ironic, but wasn't bothered by it. Henry wasn't the only one who liked to talk at, instead of to, him. Jacob was a good listener by default. And at least Henry usually gave him food for thought. Soft food, maybe, but again, that's what he liked.

He continued to sit. He didn't have to get ready. He was always ready. Jacob was "Humongo: the World's Strongest Man." That was his Circus name. Jacob thought it was kind of silly. He didn't need makeup or a colorful costume. He wore knee-length stretch pants and nothing else, to show his 'prodigious musculature'. Those were Jerry's words. Jacob had to look up 'prodigious' in the dictionary. Jerry had a way with words; he had a way with people, too. Jerry Grayling was the Ringmaster. Also, he was the owner's son. He was the boss.

Jacob had been with the Grayling Brothers' Circus since he was seventeen, more than half his life. But, even after all that time, he still felt like an outsider. Most of the people in the Circus were fifth, sixth, even seventh generation performers. Jacob and the others who came on later were treated well enough, but not like family. As big as he was, however, and as strong as he was, Jacob knew he was an asset. He knew he was appreciated, by Jerry especially.

Besides, what else was he going to do? Out in the real world, among the towners, he was a freak. He didn't fit in, sometimes literally; plus, at the Circus he was earning a living.

Also, Gwen was here. Jacob had no illusions about Gwen ever having feelings for him; he was content just to be near her. He adored Gwen. She was so beautiful and kind. Of course, everyone adored Gwen. She was their star attraction.

Every circus has standard acts, because audiences expect certain things when they go to the circus. You don't disappoint the audience. They're not just your bread and butter, but the reason you exist. Thus, standard acts: clowns; oddities; animals; jugglers; acrobats. There are more, but these five are pretty universal. Jacob was an oddity, obviously, and Gwen was an acrobat.

Not just an acrobat, though. She did tumbling, hi-wire work, trapeze work, animal work, human pyramids and pretty much anything else under the 'acrobat' umbrella.

Gwen was fearless. She would try anything, and usually with only a few rehearsals, she could master anything. She had a gift. Talented, beautiful and kind. Jacob was convinced she was an angel, on Earth to work off some sort of offense to God. Not that he could imagine her offending anyone, but God could be pretty snarky, so she might have been. An angel.

Every man in the Circus, including the married ones, and some of the women, too were in love with Gwen. If she noticed, she gave no sign. She was sweet to everyone, but sweet on no one, at least as far as Jacob could tell.

But, she was so good at her job, and drew such huge crowds, and thus money, that they were just happy to have her in the Circus.

For the most part.

There was one guy who tried to have his way with Gwen. The previous summer, this was, on a day when the temperature broke a hundred and tempers were running hot.

***

Vince was slick: good hair, easy manner, smooth voice. He was a carny, which made him a kind of cousin to the

Circus folk. He had joined them about five months before, when he was between gigs and the Circus came to the town where he was staying. He signed on to do grunt work: set-up and tear-down of tents and acts, pushing a broom, that sort of thing.

Several times, on payday, Vince would stumble back from whatever town they were playing, sometimes with a girl, sometimes a bottle, most of the time both. He got into a couple of scrapes with locals, over somebody's girlfriend, but nothing serious. Nobody was hospitalized and nobody ever called the cops. He worked hard, and he had a rough charm, so the other stuff was tolerated.

Somehow, that hot, sticky summer day, he got it into his head that he had to have Gwen. His drunk tank was about three-quarters full when he pounded on the door of her trailer, demanding to be let in, promising her the time of her life. Circus people gathered in the shadows to watch.

"Go away, Vince," her muffled voice came from inside. "You're drunk."

"A little, but I'm handsome, too," he said. "And you're beautiful. We were meant to be, baby. Plus, really, I have just got to know what you look like under that oh-so-sparkly costume."

He laughed and hit the door with his fist.

"Come on out, baby," he yelled. "Or I'm gonna bust the lock. If I have to do that, I might forget to be gentle with you."

Jacob had arrived by then, and heard these words. He stood several feet behind Vince and shook his head, unable to believe someone would ever hurt Gwen. Vince hit the door once more, harder, and said he was losing his patience.

The door opened. Gwen stood, backlit in a thin gown. Everyone could see through it and they could tell she was naked. Jacob looked away.

"Yeah," Vince said, grinning, "That's what I'm talking about. Come here, sweets. I'm going to rock your world."

"Please," Gwen said. "Don't do this. You'll regret it."

"No," said Vince. "I don't think I will. I really don't."

Vince put his left hand on her right breast, squeezing it, teasing the nipple to hardness with his thumb. Gwen watched his face, expressionless. He grinned and pinched her, hard. She gasped.

Jacob twitched, but held his ground. He didn't want to hurt anyone if he didn't have to.

"Vince," Gwen said. "There are a lot of people here. You should just go sleep it off before this gets out of hand."

"Don't you," he whispered, intense, "tell me what to do."

Gwen gave him a look of such intense fury, Vince faltered, uncertain. He changed tack, pouring on the charm.

"Come on, beautiful," he purred. "You know you want me."

"I don't want you, Vince. I find you repulsive."

Vince, eyes wide, stepped back and slapped her face with his right hand. It was loud.

"You do not get to insult me, you..." That's as far as he got.

Jacob took two strides forward and grabbed Vince by the head, pulling him away from Gwen.

"Shit! Get 'im off me!" No one moved. Vince, pulled a knife from a sheath at his belt and drove it backward into

79

Jacob's side. There was blood, but Jacob didn't seem to notice.

Jacob squeezed Vince's head, lifting him off the ground, Vince vomiting profanity and slicing at the giant again, swinging wildly. He connected twice more, but again, Jacob didn't notice. Jacob pulled Vince in close, so their bodies were touching, then his arms shot forward and whipped back. Vince's head moved too fast for his body to keep up. There was a loud 'crack'. Jacob could feel Vince's pulse under his fingers slow to a stop.

No one spoke. After a while, Jerry stepped forward.

"Jacob," he said. "This is good. You did well. We protect our own. Especially Gwen. You can put him down now. Some of the boys will make sure he goes away. Jacob, you're bleeding. You should go see Marty. He can stitch you up. He's good at that, Jacob."

Jacob listened to Jerry, of course. Jerry was the boss, but his eyes were locked on Gwen's and he waited. She nodded to him, mouthed "thank you" and went back into her trailer. Only then did Jacob drop Vince on the ground and let Marty lead him away.

Two days later, he pulled his stitches lifting a car. Some towner had bet him he couldn't do it. He won five dollars.

Since then, Gwen always had a smile for Jacob. And every time, it melted his oversized heart.

Jacob had girlfriends, though they never lasted long. His record was two months, and that was with Katya, the contortionist. Jacob was surprised to find out that was her real name; she was from Ukraine. She was also one of the few women who slept with him more than once. She was enthusiastic about sex. This was a first for him. The other women he'd slept with seemed to do it more from a sense of obligation. Jacob had to wonder if maybe that was why Katya stayed with him so long; it might also have been because she knew he was lonely and felt sorry for him. She was strange, but he enjoyed being with her. He loved having her by his side, her hand resting on his elbow as they walked around. It made him feel like a man. A normal man.

But, even during these brief relationships, Jacob's feelings for Gwen never dimmed. His love and admiration for her burned hot in his chest. He longed to tell her, but could not. Even if Jacob was capable of speech, he was too much in awe of Gwen to ever admit his feelings.

***

It was the opening day in the new spot. Jacob hadn't bothered to learn the name of the town; after a while, they all seemed the same. He saw Henry in full clown get-up come out of his trailer, do a pratt fall down the steps, nearly knocking over Marty and Madge, the midget twins. It got a laugh, even from the twins. Henry had a way of making you laugh when you were the butt of the joke. He was a good clown.

Henry passed Jacob and honked his nose in greeting. Jacob reached up and 'honked' his own in return, something he had never done. Henry laughed loudly at that.

"My god, Jacob," he said. "You developed a sense of humor!" The clown clapped him on the back with a white, padded glove. "About damn time."

Jacob had a new act: he would wrestle three men at once. If they could pin him for five seconds or knock him off the mat, they would win ten dollars. It cost a dollar each to try. Jerry told him to give the men a chance, to make them think they were winning before knocking them all off him. He was enjoying himself. These were big farm men, no weaklings, but Jacob never even broke a sweat. He had four bouts that day: twelve men total. It was a good way to make some extra money for the Circus, and Jerry gave him ten percent of it, on top of what he already earned.

Jacob didn't drink, didn't go out much, other than to the movies once in awhile. He loved the movies. There, in the dark theater, once the lights went down and everyone was watching the screen, he felt anonymous, normal. He treasured those two-hour chunks of time. So, Jacob had saved a lot of money over the years. Several thousand dollars, in fact. When he was eighteen and had been with the Circus almost a year, he came to Jerry with a large wad of cash.

***

"What's this?" Jerry asked. Jacob handed him a note he had written, explaining that these were his wages that he'd saved up and wanted to know if Jerry could keep them safe somewhere. Jacob had no idea where to put the money, but he knew it was important to keep it.

"You saved all this?" Jerry was incredulous. Jacob nodded. No teenager in his experience could resist spending his money. "Okay," he continued. "Here's what we'll do. Some banks have branches all over the U.S. We'll get you a savings account, put the money in there, and whenever you want, you can put money in or take money out. Sound good?"

Jacob nodded again, trusting him. As it turns out, it was trust well-placed. Jerry got him the account, and over the years, it accumulated a large balance. Jacob wasn't rich, by any means, but he could take a few years off if he wanted and still not run out of money. He didn't want to. He was just as strong as ever, and leaving the Circus would mean being away from Gwen.

***

Gwen, who was still performing daring acrobatics. Gwen, who was beautiful and fearless. Gwen, who had been with the Circus when Jacob signed on sixteen years ago. Gwen, who still looked like she was nineteen.

It hit Jacob only now. Gwen never changed. She never got sick, or hurt, or made a mistake in her routines. Never got any older. My god, he thought, she really *is* an angel. He sped to his trailer and grabbed pen and paper. The pen was tiny in his hand, but he was used to that. And he only needed to write a few words. He went to see Gwen, knocked gently on her trailer door.

She opened the door, smiled at him. She was so lovely.

"Hello, Jacob. What can I do for you?" He handed her the note.

It said "I know your secret. Don't be afraid. I won't tell anyone."

"How did you find out, Jacob? Did someone tell you?" He shook his head no. "Figured it out on your own, did you? You're so very clever, my friend." She beamed at him. "Won't you come in?" He nodded. It was tight, but he didn't bang his head or knock anything over.

"Well, Jacob," she said. "What do we do now? This is something we mustn't tell anyone else. You know that, right?"

Jacob nodded again. She could trust him; surely she knew that.

"Good. I have an idea. Since you know what I am, you can help me."

Jacob was very pleased. He would do anything for Gwen.

"I knew I could count on you, Jacob. You're so good to me. I'll let you know when I need you, okay?"

Jacob nodded. When she needed him. Gwen, needing him. He grinned all the way back to his trailer. He was still grinning when he picked up his dumbbells to work out. Henry walked by, out of his clown costume, but still wearing make-up. His red nose was in his hand.

"That's a tad unnerving," he said. "A giant curling eighty pounds in each hand and grinning like the cat that ate the canary." Jacob shrugged, still smiling. He did another ten reps with each arm. Henry watched his biceps flex.

"You know what I like about you, Jacob? You're the real deal. No tricks, no gimmicks, just a big, strong guy. You know how rare that is in the Circus? Most of us are full of shit." He watched Jacob do a few more reps. "Nice talking to you, as always."

Henry walked off. Jacob worked out for another forty minutes or so, then went to his trailer to shower. His good mood lasted for days.

It was another two weeks before Gwen asked him for help.

***

Jacob had just defeated four large men, construction workers, on the big mat. It was a good fight; they worked together and pinned him down, but he was up again in three seconds, throwing one of them right off the mat. He tossed the other three off the mat with little difficulty. It was the closest he'd ever come to losing, and it was invigorating. Jacob turned to the crowd after the last opponent was done and he flexed and grinned. They cheered for him. Yeah, he thought, I could get used to that. He saw Gwen by the tent flap. When he caught her eye, she smiled and clapped her hands.

When the show was over, she was waiting for him.

"Jacob, come to my trailer tonight after dark. The time has come for you to help me." He nodded. "You're so strong, Jacob. And you have such energy. I've never seen you fight before. It was impressive."

He flushed from her praise, smiled and shrugged. It was just how he was, he wanted to say.

"See you tonight, big guy." She walked away, leaving him happier than he'd ever been. He could hardly wait for nightfall.

To pass the time, Jacob went for a walk. He left the Circus and headed to town. There were still at least a couple of hours of daylight left; he would try to catch a movie if there was a theater in town. There wasn't, but there was a man playing guitar on the sidewalk, his empty case in front of him, some change and a dollar bill in there. He played well, a bluesy and pretty song, and Jacob stopped to listen for a while. The man smiled at him, showing gaps in his teeth. While he listened, Jacob played various scenarios in his mind about what might happen at Gwen's. He really didn't know what to expect, but could think of some very nice possibilities. After a couple songs, Jacob tossed a couple of tens in the case and moved on.

"Thank you! God Bless You!" Jacob nodded to him and kept going. It felt good to surprise people, to help them out. And he did feel blessed. That made him think of Gwen again. He headed back to the Circus.

He ran into one of the men he'd fought earlier, and nodded at him. It was all in good fun, right, he tried to say with his eyes. It didn't seem to work. From behind his back, the man pulled out half a broom handle and slapped it into his other palm. From a nearby doorway came the other three he had beaten. They had sticks, too. They surrounded him. The first one spoke.

"Let's see how you do now, tough guy. Let's see how you do when there's no mat and no rules. Freak." He swung his stick. Jacob turned and took it on his lats. His 'prodigious musculature' absorbed it with ease. Two more hits came in, one on his shoulder, the other just above the knee. Lucky. Another, immediately after grazed his head. Jacob felt no pain. His adrenaline kicked in and everything slowed down.

Jacob hunched, head down and let them hit him one more time. They were almost synchronized. On their backswing, he raised his head, targeted the first man, the one who called him a freak and let fly with his fist. Jacob was fast, and the man never had a chance. Jacob knocked him out and broke his face.

He whirled, catching another man with his left hand in the gut. It sent the man back six feet. The other two paused. Jacob did not. He grabbed one by the head with his right hand, spun him around and used him as a club to hit his friend. Both went down.

The fight was over in seven seconds, and the men were lucky to be alive. Jacob had the beginnings of a bruise on his thigh, and his head was seeping blood from a small cut. He felt fine. He felt great. Physically. He also felt bad for hurting the men, even though he was defending himself, and they were armed. He looked around, afraid of getting in trouble, afraid of getting the Circus in trouble.

"It's all right, big fella," a man said nearby. "I saw them attack you, and I was there when you beat them the first time. Anyone asks, I've got your back."

Jacob nodded his thanks, grateful.

"You don't talk much, do you?" Jacob shook his head, pointing to his throat. "Ah. I see. Mute, then. Guess when you're as big as you, you don't need to talk." Jacob shook his head again. "All right. You get on back, big fella, before this scene draws a crowd. I'll walk over to the town doctor and let him know these here gentlemen need medical assistance. I'll take my time, I think. It's such a nice night."

Jacob smiled at him and the man smiled back. They both walked away from the unconscious four. When Jacob got back, the sun was setting. He washed the blood off his head and the sweat and dirt off the rest of him and went to see Gwen.

When Jacob knocked on her trailer door, she told him to come in. When he did, he was confused and embarrassed. Gwen had a man with her, under her. They were naked, sweaty. Gwen smiled at him.

"It's okay, silly. Come in and close the door." Not knowing what else to do, Jacob came in. The man didn't seem to notice him. He stared up at Gwen, enraptured. Jacob couldn't turn away, though he hated what he saw; hated that his body reacted to it. Gwen focused once more on the man below her, moving her body on his.

The man climaxed, his body convulsing. Then, he deflated, his body collapsing into itself. And Gwen glowed. Light came from her skin. Moments later, she stopped glowing and sat smiling on the flesh covered bones that was once a man.

"You look shocked, Jacob," she said. "You said you knew what I was."

Jacob shook his head. This wasn't right. She was an angel.

"I am an angel, Jacob," she said, reading his thoughts. "Or I was anyway. I kind of fell. Just a little. I'm a succubus. I have sex with men and suck the life out of them. It keeps me young and pretty. Plus, it's fun!"

Jacob shook his head. This wasn't possible. This was not the Gwen he loved.

"I know it's a lot to process, Jacob," she said. "But, I need your help. You are so big and strong. You have so much energy. Help me, Jacob. I need you."

Jacob looked into her eyes and was lost.

She stood and shoved the other man's remains off the bed with her foot. They hit the floor with the soft clatter of dice in a bag.

Gwen lay on the bed and he came to her, knowing it was crazy, knowing he was going to die and not caring. He would give her anything, his angel. He loved her so much.

He climbed on top of her, careful not to crush her. It was perfect. He had the best sex of his life that night. When he finished, he felt like a god. Then he was gone.

He was the world's strongest man, and he was tasty and very filling.

Making a Splash

Jim leaned back from staring at the Falls, glancing at the people around him. He counted three couples, honeymooning, and two old men, seventy or so. The only sound was the constant roar of water, drowning everything else out.

Jim sang under his breath: *when that shark bites with his teeth, dear; Scarlet billows, they begin to spread.* One hand rested on the handle of The Knife. The blade was still sheathed, out of sight beneath his jacket. The handle was wood, old, worn, and smooth. It felt good in Jim's hand, but not like before. Nothing like before. It was like it was sleeping now. That *connection* was gone.

Jim watched the rainbows in the mist. The Falls really were beautiful. He'd seen pictures, movies, too, but it didn't compare to being right there.

One of the young men pulled his bride close and kissed her. There was real passion in that kiss.

Jim reflected on the last year or so. He'd been busy. Too busy to think about what he was doing. Now that it was over, he was thinking. He was remembering. He wished he wasn't.

One of the old men laughed, but there was no sound; it was like watching TV with the mute button on. The pretty girl, the one between him and the old man was looking at him. He caught her eye and smiled at her. She smiled back then turned away, shy.

It was odd: Jim had no desire to kill her at all.

Jim turned away from her. He noticed that one of the couples was now a single. The young woman had gone inside; Jim could just see her passing through the door. Her husband caught Jim's eye and nodded a greeting. Seeing something in the man's eye, something approachable, Jim walked over to him.

"Jim!" he shouted.

"No! Carl!" the other yelled back. Jim smiled at him.

"No! I mean me! I'm Jim! Nice to meet you, Carl!"

Carl leaned back and laughed, mute button on. Carl put out his hand, and instead of shaking it, Jim pulled out The Knife, still in its sheath and pressed it into Carl's palm. Carl felt a shock, like static electricity; he jumped a bit.

"What's this?" he yelled into Jim's ear.

"An ending, Carl. And, I suspect, a beginning, too." Jim paused, took Carl by the shoulders and leaned back to look him in the eye. He moved in again to be heard.

"I killed one hundred people with that Knife. One hundred on the nose. It took me a long time." Carl was speechless. Jim gave his shoulder an affectionate squeeze and smiled at him. He leaned in one more time to shout.

"Anyway," Jim said, grinning as the perfect line occurred to him, "it's out of my hands now!" And with that, Jim leaped over the rail. He looked at the rainbows all the way down. Lovely.

***

Carl and Julie sat on the bed in their hotel room. The Knife sat on the bed between them.

"My god." Julie was shaken. "One hundred people? Why did he give it to you?"

"I... have no idea."

Julie stared at The Knife.

"This is evidence or something, isn't it? We should call the cops."

"I don't think so," Carl said.

"Why not?"

"My fingerprints are on it now, and the real killer is gone."

"Then, we need to get rid of it. Throw it over the falls, too."

"I have a better idea."

"What?"

Carl reached for his new wife, pulling her close. She was surprised, but moved into him. He kissed her a while and pulled back a little.

"You're horny? Now?"

"No. Maybe. Kind of. I'm, I don't know, energized, I guess. It's hard to explain."

"You're being weird, Carl."

"I'm sorry. I love you. You have to know that."

"Of course I do," Julie said. "I love you, too."

Carl pulled The Knife from its sheath, making a small scraping sound. He gently but firmly slid The Knife in between her ribs and into her heart. He watched the blade go in, watched the blood slowly seep out around the hand-guard. Julie gasped, eyes opening wide. She looked down at his hands, one holding The Knife, the other resting on her thigh.

The hands she had always admired for their strength and grace, the hands of her new husband.

"Sh. It's okay, Julie. It's okay. The first one is always the hardest. It's going to get so much easier from now on. Only ninety-nine to go. That's not so many. Not so many at all."

Carl watched the humanity fade from Julie's eyes. When she was gone, Carl felt the first piece on a hundred piece puzzle snap into place. Carl cleaned The Knife on her shirt, took a shower and put on clean clothes. Carl kissed his dead wife on the cheek and set fire to the hotel.

He sang softly to himself as he went to look for number two. *Someone's sneaking 'round the corner. Could that someone, perhaps, perchance, be Mack the Knife?*

TOM'S PERSONAL DEMONS

"Wait," Tom said, an edge of panic in his voice. Carla turned to look at him, her fingers on the lamp's brass toggle switch. She caught his eyes flick up to meet hers. Carla thought he had been looking at her thigh. To be fair, she was showing a lot of leg.

"Please," Tom said, "leave it on. I have a… thing." He shrugged. Carla's lips twitched in a half smile.

"You're afraid of the dark?"

"I didn't say that," Tom said. "But, yeah. That about sums it up."

Carla looked Tom Branson over. She mentally filed this new information with everything else she knew about the man. There wasn't a lot. Though they had been dating for a couple weeks, this was the first time she'd seen him without his clothes on.

Tom was good-looking, or he wouldn't be in her bed. She was honest enough to admit that, shallow though it may be. A woman must have standards after all. Tom had a nice body: he obviously worked out, but he wasn't one of those chiseled boys who spent all day at the gym and ate nine eggs with a side of steroids for breakfast. Tom had a nice penis, too: not at all small, but it didn't look like it would get so big you'd run screaming.

So, he was afraid of the dark. *Everybody has issues*, Carla thought. So far, she had quite enjoyed his company. She let her eyes roam over Tom as he lay naked on her bed, one corner of the sheet covering most of his left leg and nothing else. Tom's body reacted to her scrutiny and Carla raised an eyebrow.

"I think," she said, dropping her voice an octave, "I'm okay with the light being on." Carla gave Tom a smile full of mischief and dragged the oversized tank top over her head. She wore nothing under it. Carla watched Tom's eyes. This was the first time he'd seen her naked, too. His appreciation was visibly growing.

She didn't run, but there was some screaming.

Later, breathless and slippery, Carla rolled off Tom and flopped onto the bed on her back. Both of them were grinning and panting like they'd just finished a race. If it was a race, they tied for first place. A lot of guys hit the finish line way before she was even halfway there.

When he had caught his breath, Tom sat up, turned away from Carla and surreptitiously removed the condom. He looked around the room, then at Carla.

"Um," he said. "Garbage can?" Carla reached down next to the bed and held up a small, dark green metal can with a white plastic shopping bag lining it. Tom tossed the condom in among the few used tissues and dust bunnies; Carla had swept the floor in her room earlier. To Carla, the rubber looked like a deflated balloon that was left forgotten in the basement after the party had been over for days.

"That," she said, grinning at Tom, "was some pretty great sex." Tom grinned back. He nodded.

"Yeah," he said. "It really was." Carla gave him a sleepy smile. She wondered if she should ask him to stay. She wasn't sure if she wanted him to. Spending the night with a man implied some kind of commitment. Of course, so did sex.

Carla propped herself up on her elbows. She knew this position made her breasts look great. Tom noticed. Carla savored his appreciation for a moment. Then, she sat up, took his hand and held it in hers. She kissed Tom's palm, a gesture that almost felt as intimate as having him inside her. She met his eyes.

"You want some water?" Carla said. "I'm totally thirsty." Tom nodded and they both got up. Carla pulled on her tank which fell to mid-thigh. Tom followed her cue, pulling on his boxers and his pants. He buckled his belt, but left his shirt off. It was comfortably warm in Carla's house.

Carla led Tom to the kitchen and poured them both glasses of water from the filtered pitcher in the fridge. They drank without speaking until both glasses were empty. Tom set his glass carefully on the counter by the sink. Carla put hers next to it. Tom looked like he was about to say something, but Carla spoke first.

"You could stay," she said, "if you want, I mean."

"I, uh," Tom started. "That'd be nice, but..."

"I'll leave the light on, Tom," Carla said. Tom smiled, a big, warm, genuine smile.

"Deal," said Tom, putting out his hand. Absurdly, they shook on it.

They both brushed their teeth with her toothbrush and paste. Tom hadn't expected to stay, so he didn't have his. Carla took out her contacts and put them in the case. She squinted at Tom.

"You're still cute," she said, "even blurry."

"I didn't know you wore contacts," Tom said.

"Nearsighted," Carla said. "I tried glasses, but I hate the way they feel on my face.

"I've been lucky," Tom said. "I've always had good vision." Carla yawned.

"I'm pretty tired, Tom," Carla said. He nodded. They returned to the well-lit bedroom.

Tom lay down and held the sheet for her. Carla climbed in next to him, turned her back on Tom and the lamp and snuggled into him. He reached across her, sliding his arm under hers and across her chest. Hand on her shoulder, he held her to him.

Carla lay there for a while, listening to Tom breathe. She was trying to determine if he was awake, but wasn't sure. She whispered his name and he hummed a syllable in reply.

"When did it start?" Carla asked. Tom propped himself on his elbow. She turned to look at him. His eyes were alert. He had been awake after all.

"My thing about the dark?" he asked. Carla nodded. "I don't remember exactly. I was a kid, obviously. Six, maybe seven years old. I've never told anyone about this except my shrink." Carla didn't say anything. She didn't want to scare him off, and she was curious. She'd never met an adult who was still afraid of the dark.

Carla pushed an errant hair behind Tom's ear. She loved that he wore it unfashionably long.

Tom took a breath and let it out. Carla's face was inches from his and she could smell beer on his breath under the toothpaste. It was an odd combination, though not entirely unpleasant.

"My mom used to turn off the light," Tom was saying, "and close the door. My bed was about eight feet away from the switch; it might as well have been a mile. I would lie there in the dark, terrified to move, or make a sound. After a few seconds in the dark, red dots would appear in the air above and around me. This happened pretty much every night. At first, they looked kind of cool, floating around my room. But, then-"

He stopped. Carla saw naked terror on Tom's face for a second. He was clearly reliving something awful. He closed his eyes and took deep breaths. When he opened them, he seemed calm again.

"But, then," he started again, "the red dots would always become eyes, and faces would form around the eyes. Hideous, malevolent faces surrounded me, sneering, leering, snarling, insane demons. I only ever saw their faces; they may have had bodies, too, but if they did, they were hidden in the dark."

"Jesus," Carla said. "No wonder you were scared. You had one hell of an imagination." Tom's hair had fallen again, so Carla tucked it back, her fingers lingering on his cheek. Tom looked up and Carla was surprised to see tears on the brink of his lower lids.

"I'm convinced they're still there," he said, "in the dark. I can feel them watching me, waiting for the lights to go out."

"Wow," Carla said. She held his gaze, trying not to let Tom see that she was wondering if maybe she had let a crazy person into her house, into her bed.

"You probably think I'm nuts," Tom said with a small, forced laugh. "Wouldn't blame you."

"No," Carla said. "I think maybe you never outgrew an overactive imagination." Tom smiled at her. He leaned in and kissed her on the cheek. *Not enough men do that*, Carla thought.

"Goodnight, Tom," she said. "I'm glad you stayed." Tom hugged her to him and said he was glad, too.

Somehow, Carla managed to fall asleep with the light on, though it took much longer than usual.

***

Carla said she was sorry mid-yawn, but Heather waved Carla's apology away. They were having a late lunch, sitting close enough to hear one another in the noisy bar. Heather was on her second Manhattan; Carla was drinking coffee. Her coffee consumption had more than doubled in the last month.

At two in the afternoon, except for a large group against the wall, Carla and Heather had the place to themselves. They liked to meet in Gary's Place because it was off the beaten path and tourists didn't know about it. Neither woman was very tolerant of tourists, but like most Bostonians, they were both friendly when you met them one on one.

Once a sunburned, sweating, badly dressed idiot stopped gawking at the historic sights with their camera glued to their face, they became human again and you could stand being in the same room with them.

This particular afternoon, however, Gary's Place was hosting a retirement party for Stanley. The two women knew it was Stanley's party; his name was shouted over twenty times in the first five minutes. It looked to Carla like the entire company had come out to see Stanley off. Carla wondered if the company was footing the bar tab.

Carla and Heather watched the folks for a while, but the longer it went on, and the more Stanley's soon-to-be-former co-workers drank, the louder it got in there. They could no longer talk without shouting. Heather signaled the waiter; the two women split the bill and left.

Outside, the sun reflected and amplified off the skyscraper windows, cooking the street. Thankfully, the breeze abated the heat somewhat, and the relative quiet after

Stanley's party was sublime. Carla and Heather stood on the sidewalk for a moment and listened to the gulls scream at each other.

Heather finally turned to Carla with a face that said it would brook no bullshit.

"You look like shit, girl," Heather said. "What the hell is going on?" Carla sighed. She stifled another in a long series of yawns.

"I told you Tom moved in, right?" Carla began. Heather nodded. "He'd be so pissed if he knew I was telling you this, but I gotta tell somebody. I'm losing my damn mind."

"What?" Heather said. "Is he doing something illegal? Are you in trouble?" Heather was always ready to rescue Carla from all threats, be they real or imagined.

"No, no," Carla said. "Nothing like that. Tom's, um, Tom's afraid of the dark. No. Don't laugh. It's serious: a crippling phobia. He can't handle the lights being out."

"Why don't you get a sleeping mask?" Heather asked.

"I tried," Carla said. "It was like wearing glasses, only worse, because I was trying to sleep. I hate having anything on my face."

"I remember that," Heather said She suddenly snorted. "How old is Tom, anyway?" Carla wanted to slap the derision off her friend's face.

"Shut up, Heather," Carla said. "He's embarrassed by it, but can't help it. Tom's got this incredible imagination. He's really creative and he's quick and funny. He's cute and thoughtful and affectionate. When I was sick, he bought me stuffed animals to cheer me up. Who does that? And, he loves me. I love him, too. He's everything I could want in a man, but... He's been living with me for the last month. I'm not getting much sleep, and I'm so damn tired all the time."

Heather stared out at the bay, thinking. Carla watched a woman pull a double stroller with twin toddlers in it up a set of marble steps. The tendons in the mother's forearms rippled like cables under the skin. Carla was about to offer the woman help when Heather spoke.

"The stuffed animal thing is pretty cool," Heather said. "I'm sorry I laughed, Carla. Tom sounds great. Pretty much. Has he seen a shrink?"

"Yes," Carla said, "Nine of them over the years." Heather nodded. She looked back at the water. Carla checked on the struggling mother; the woman was now on the top step. The stroller was one step down. One of the boys pulled his finger out of his nose. He offered the boogers to his brother, who ate it. *Gross*, Carla thought. *Funny, but gross.* She glanced at Heather. Heather met her eyes and smirked.

"Maybe number ten will do the trick," Heather said.

***

Tom and Carla were eating in their favorite restaurant in the North End. The lights were so low it was almost hard to see the next table. But not so low that Tom had a problem. An empty Champagne bottle lay face-down in a bucket of mostly melted ice. Their desserts, chocolate cheesecake for her, gelato for him, lay massacred on small china plates by their espresso cups. Carla patted her stomach and gave Tom a sleepy, dopey smile. She would have to do an extra mile at the gym tomorrow.

"Happy anniversary, beautiful," Tom said. "Hard to believe it's been a year." Carla smiled at him. She didn't feel beautiful, and was glad the lights were low. The dimness, along with carefully applied makeup, masked the bags under her eyes. Carla thought she would eventually get used to sleeping with the light on, but she hadn't yet.

Tom reached for his tiny porcelain cup and knocked his spoon off the table. He slid his chair back and knelt to pick it up. From one knee, he looked up at Carla. Her eyes went wide. She knew this pose, but was totally unprepared for it.

"You're not-," Carla began, but stopped. From nowhere, Tom produced a small, dark gray jewelry case. He opened it with his other hand. Inside, a bright red ruby, her favorite stone, was set in white gold with diamond chips that caught the meager light. It was modest, but gorgeous. Carla's heart thumped against her ribs; she held her breath as she waited for him to speak.

"Carla," Tom whispered. He cleared his throat. "Will you marry me?" For just a second, Carla had a flash of years and years of sleeping with the light on and nearly panicked. But, she loved him. He was perfect, except for that one tiny flaw.

She said yes.

***

The week before the wedding, Carla and Heather waited for the other women to show up. It was a low-key affair, this bachelorette party. No dancing cop with Velcro pants, washboard abs and a thong. Just nine very close friends, a private beach and an open bar. Heather jabbed Carla in the ribs a little hard. Carla rubbed the sore spot and grimaced at her best friend.

"One more week of freedom," Heather said. "You'll still call me once in awhile, right?"

"I'm getting married," Carla said, "not joining the French Foreign Legion."

"How are you going to survive the rest of your life with the light on, honey?" Heather was suddenly serious. Carla shook her head. It was a question Carla had asked herself many times. She hadn't been able to come up with an answer, but she was determined to make it work.

She was spared having to field any more questions by the arrival of Kate and Vanessa who must have carpooled. More women showed up in ones or two quickly after that. The rest of the night was filled with hugs and drinks and laughter and more hugs.

A couple of hours in, Carla wondered if Tom was having fun at his party. They had decided to have them on the same night. He told her he wasn't going to have a stripper either, but Carla wasn't worried either way. She knew he was loyal to her. And, in almost two years, she was pretty sure he had never lied to her. Not even the dumb stuff everybody lies about.

How you feeling today, honey?

Not great, actually. I have some bad gas pains.

Carla put Tom, the wedding and everything else out of her head and kept a steady buzz throughout the night. She drank and laughed at Brandy Williams, who really should have been a stand-up comic instead of a high school teacher. It was pretty much a perfect night.

***

Carla looked over at her husband, her heart as full of love for him as her womb was with his child. She had done the math: she must have gotten pregnant on, or very shortly after their wedding night. Pretty much as soon as they stopped using condoms. Carla ran her hand over her belly; she felt a flutter and then a foot pushed on her hand. It was like her baby knew where her hand was. Maybe he did. Carla wanted a boy, but they both wanted to be surprised. She thought of the baby as *he*.

"How you doin', honey?" Tom asked. He asked her this several times a day. She couldn't blame him; her answer changed a lot.

"I'm happy," she said. "Tired, but happy." Tom smiled.

"You're always tired," he said. "But, I'm glad you're happy. You know I love you." Carla nodded.

"I love you, too." A serious expression came over Tom's face. She raised an eyebrow.

"I want to do something for you," Tom said. "With the baby coming, I think we need to make a change."

"What kind of change, Tom?"

"I don't want our baby to inherit my... issues," Tom said. "I want to try sleeping in the dark. I think it's time." Carla wiggled herself into a sitting position, a task that took the better part of a minute. With a finger, she brushed an errant lock of Tom's hair behind his ear. She searched his face for a long time.

"Really?" Carla said. "Are you sure? I mean-" She stopped. They both knew what she meant.

"I'm as sure as I'm ever going to be," Tom said. "If I'm going to be a father, I need to start acting like one. I have to face my fear if I'm ever going to get over it."

"I can't tell you," Carla said, "how long I've waited to hear you say that. I'm so proud of you, honey!" Carla hugged her husband as well as she could; her massive middle made it awkward. He hugged her back, firm but gentle, too.

They read for a while: Tom, a Neil Gaiman novel he loved so much he'd already read twice; Carla, a baby name book. She was torn between Thomas Jr. and Martin, after her father. She knew Tom wanted to name their baby Bruce, after Bruce Campbell, or Stephanie if it was a girl. Carla wasn't even looking at girls' names. She glanced over at Tom. He had let himself go, but just a little; he had a tiny paunch going over his pajama bottoms. Carla had heard that a lot of men gained weight when their wives were pregnant. She was going to lose as much as she could as soon as she could start working out again. Maybe Tom would lose his, too. Or, maybe not; it was kind of cute, she thought. Love the man, love the whole package, right? Besides, Carla had a whole lot more middle than Tom right now, so who was she to judge?

Carla noticed Tom was looking back. She smiled at him, and he returned it.

"What's up?" he asked.

"When did you think," Carla asked, "you might want to start trying the lights out thing? No pressure. I was just curious."

"Tonight," Tom said. "Let's dive right in. Why not, right?" Carla nodded. They were quiet for a minute or so.

"So," Carla said, "my midwife says it's safe to have sex all the way up to labor. Just, you know, f.y.i."

"You sure I wouldn't give the little guy a concussion?" Tom laughed.

"You're not *that* big!" Carla playfully slapped Tom on the arm. They were both laughing. Before much longer, however, they were side-by-side, carefully, but enthusiastically making love.

Later, after Tom got them water from the kitchen, he kissed her and told her he loved her.

"Back atcha," Carla grunted, trying to find a comfortable way to settle her bulk. Tom reached over and put his hand on the lamp. Carla watched him. He hesitated, turned to Carla and grinned at her.

"Here goes nothing," he said, and turned out the light. The click of the toggle echoed in Carla's ears.

Carla listened in the darkness. She could hear the fridge humming in the kitchen. She could hear the bathroom sink drip every few seconds. Tom had checked out a basic plumbing book from the library, but he didn't have the right wrench, so the damn thing still dripped.

Outside, a car went by slowly, its tires crunching on the gravel road. Carla had come to enjoy that sound over the years. She also liked that her non-paved road got a lot less traffic; being on the brink of having a child had made her hyper-aware of these sorts of things.

Tom lay next to her, his breathing changing to short, gasping bursts. Carla could feel his body grow tense. She reached back with her hand and held his. He squeezed her fingers a little too hard.

"Do you see anything?" Carla whispered. She was hoping for a no.

"Red dots," Tom said, his normal speaking voice very loud in the dark. "So far, just red dots. You don't see them?" Carla opened her eyes and saw nothing but the thin line of light under the door to the hall.

"Sorry, honey," she said. "I don't see any dots. But, I'm here, you know. I'm here for you, Tom." She stroked the back of his hand with a finger. Inside, her baby woke up and worked on perfecting a circus act.

"I know, baby," Tom said. "I'll be okay. It's all in my head." Despite his brave words, Tom cringed beside her.

Carla stroked his hand faster and made shushing, comforting noises.

"They're eyes now," Tom whispered. "It's just like old times." He tried to laugh at his joke, but failed.

"You can do this, honey," Carla said. "I'm right here. I've got you."

Tom was shaking so hard the headboard was tapping the wall. Carla could smell rank fear sweat coming off of him. *Jesus,* she thought. *He's terrified!* She worked her finger on the back of his hand again and again, willing her husband to calm down. It didn't work.

"Shit," Tom nearly shouted, startling Carla. The baby stopped moving. "They're faces now, Carla. They're just as ugly as I remember. No. Uglier. Oh, fuck. I think they heard me."

Tom let go of her hand and pushed himself up until he was sitting against the headboard. Another car went by.

"Honey?" Carla said. "What can I do?" The bed shook a little; Tom was either nodding or shaking his head. She couldn't tell which.

"Do you want to turn on the light?" she continued.

"No," Tom said, but she could tell he didn't mean it. "I mean, yes, I do, but I have to do this. It's not real. Right?"

"Right."

Something scurried across Carla's thigh, startling her. *We don't have a cat,* she thought. *Do we?*

Next to her Tom whimpered. To Carla, he sounded like a little kid. Another something scampered over her foot. She gave a little cry.

"You see them?" Tom demanded. "You see them!"

106

"No," Carla said. "I don't see anything, but I thought I felt something-" Tom panicked. He screamed and thrashed. He struck out blindly and one of his fists connected with Carla's left eye. White, hot light exploded behind her eye and she lurched away from him.

Carla fell off the bed, and her baby flipped inside her as she came down on her knee. Carla cried out in pain as her kneecap cracked against the floor. There was a sickening crunching sound on impact, and she nearly fell on her face, too, but got a hand out in time.

Behind her, Carla could hear scurrying sounds and another sound she didn't recognize. It sounded a little like dice being knocked together. Suddenly, her nose was filled with the foul scent of fresh piss. *Tom wet the bed,* she thought. *Poor guy. He'll be so embarrassed.*

Carla crawled, awkwardly using her hands and only one knee toward the door. The light at the bottom was the only thing she could see. It seemed to take forever to get there. Behind her, Tom screamed again and again, pain and terror battling for supremacy; both sounded like they were doing terrible things to his throat. Through the screams, Carla could still hear the dice clicking noise and something else. A ripping sound. It made her think of pulling the meat off a chicken after it's been cooked.

Carla reached the hall door, already exhausted. Her knee felt twice its normal size. *Matches my ankles now*, she barked a laugh. She sounded hysterical to her own ears. Carla sat up against the wall and reached up to grab the doorknob. She twisted it and pushed.

Light spilled in from the hall. For an instant, the room was frozen in tableau. On the bed, Tom lay on his back, head and shoulders propped on the headboard. He was bleeding from several deep cuts all over. Chunks of flesh were missing from most of his body. His penis was severed near the base; it flopped toward Carla, hanging by a piece of skin. Blood pulsed out of the part still attached to Tom in rhythmic spurts. One of his fingers was only bone. His ring finger on his left hand, Carla realized. She took it all in with a shudder of revulsion and horror.

Then, she saw them. In that flash of light from the hall, Tom's personal demons turned to her. They had short, blunt teeth; blood spattered their tiny, hellish faces. As one, they turned their red eyes on Carla. Several looked ready to spring. Carla's bladder let go and piss spread out on the floor beneath her. It smelled like panic.

Carla groped on the wall, trying to get up, and her fingers hit something. The overhead light switch. She glanced back at the bed and the cat-sized demons were bounding across the room toward her, hungry red eyes locked on her own.

Carla fumbled for the switch again, but she had lost it. She wouldn't look away from the advancing monsters. She knew they'd get her if she took her eyes off them.

They got to the edge of the light coming in from the door and stopped. They couldn't, or wouldn't leave the shadows. Carla looked away to find the switch. *There it is!* She twisted her cumbersome body to reach it, and a sudden, horrible pain in her calf brought her up short. Her leg had slid into the shadow and one of the monsters had bitten her. Carla yanked her leg back into the light and glared at the one who'd done it. It lolled out a short, black tongue like a pug's and licked her blood off its lips.

"F-fuck you," Carla said. The little monster grabbed its groin with a clawed hand and thrust it at her. Bile rose in Carla's throat.

Making sure no part of her went into the shadows this time, Carla carefully reached for the light switch. She couldn't reach it. Carla's baby got the hiccups inside her and she despaired he would be killed along with her. She started to cry.

Sudden light filled the room from the bedside lamp, hurting Carla's already sore eye even more. Tom's hand was still on the switch and his pain ridden eyes found those of his pregnant wife. Their tiny, monstrous heads whipped back toward him.

The demons screamed, a tortured sound that would stay with Carla for the rest of her life. They seemed rooted to the spot in the light. There they stood, tiny bodies rigid, seemingly paralyzed by the light. They twitched and spasmed, then started to smolder. Then, they started to smoke and finally they burned.

Carla counted them. Fourteen little flaming monsters on the floor. She watched them burn down to ash. The fire didn't spread at all. Not even to the throw rug two of them were on. Carla looked at Tom. He was a mess.

"I love you," Tom said, his voice a wreck. "I'm sorry, baby. I didn't think they would be real for you." Carla shook her head. She pushed her back against the wall and tried to stand. This act was hard over enough the last month or so, but with the broken knee and bleeding calf on the opposite leg, it proved impossible. Instead, Carla scooted on her butt to the bed. She slid through five piles of ash on the way. She wanted to call 911, but the nearest phone was two rooms away.

"We should get you to the hospital," Carla said. She held Tom's right hand, the one with all the fingers.

"I don't think it'll help," Tom said. "It's okay, though. I finally faced my fears. After all this time, I did it. I hope it's a boy, honey. I know how badly you want a boy."

"If it is, I'll name him Bruce," Carla said. Tears ran freely down her face. Tom gave her a weak smile.

"If it's a girl," he began. His eyes closed. His chest stopped moving for a few seconds, then suddenly he inhaled. Tom opened his eyes and tried to focus on her.

"Stephanie," Clara said. "If it's a girl, I'll name her Stephanie."

"Pretty," Tom said. "Wish I'd thought of it." His eyes closed again. Clara held his hand on the blood-soaked bed and watched her husband breathe his last breath. She lay her head on his chest and cried and cried.

Carla may never have moved, but her water broke, soaking her legs and the carpet. *Perfect.*

Carla forced herself to crawl to the door. She scooted and pulled herself across the floor, left knee and right calf protesting at every movement. After what seemed like forever, Carla reached the kitchen where she'd left her phone.

She hit the speed dial button for 911. After two rings, they answered, asking her to state her emergency.

"My husband is dead," she said fast, "and I'm about to have my baby."

"Ma'am," the operator said, "is this for real?"

***

Carla closed the book and kissed Stephanie on the cheek. The girl wrapped her small arms around her mother's neck and kissed her back.

"One more story, Mama?" Stephanie said. She always wanted one more. Carla shook her head.

"We already did three, baby," she told her daughter. Carla pulled the covers up to Stephanie's neck. She brushed the hair behind her daughter's ear; the act, and the girl's hair reminded her so much of Tom.

"Mama?" Stephanie said.

"Mm-hmm?" Carla was already thinking of the novel she was currently reading and a glass of wine.

"Lucy says it's weird to sleep with the light on."

"Is Lucy a girl from school?" Carla asked.

"Uh-huh, she's my best friend in the whole world!" Stephanie's arms shot out to the sides to show how big this news really was. Carla smiled at her.

"Let's turn them off for a bit," Carla said. "Okay?"

"Okay, Mama." Carla turned off the lights. The only light in the room came from the streetlight outside their apartment; it fell in a rectangle on the floor.

"What do you see, Steph?" Carla whispered.

"Red dots," Stephanie said. "They're kind of pretty, but kind of scary, too." Carla turned on the light.

"Those are Daddy's monsters, honey," she told her daughter. "As long as the light is on, they can't hurt you. Daddy and I found this out the hard way. I'll never let them get you. Do you understand?" Stephanie nodded.

"I love you, Mama," she said.

"I love you, too, baby," Carla said. "Now, get some sleep, so you can grow big and strong."

Carla left the light on, went to the kitchen and poured two glasses of wine. She drained one right away and made the second one last. She opened the cupboard and checked the supply.

Fifty light bulbs. Over a hundred candles of varying sizes and colors. Nine high-powered flashlights.

Might have to go the store soon.

First Case of the Year

"Ten. Nine. Eight. Seven. Six. Five. Four. Three. Two. ONE!!! Happy New Year!" Thirty five voices called out in near harmony. Nice. Then, the obligatory hugs, kisses and handshakes all around. Same shit, different year.

Five minutes later, my phone rang. If I hadn't had it on vibrate, I never would have noticed. Why in the hell did I put it on vibrate?

After I got off the phone, I called Sam, my partner. At least we were both still sober. Close enough to fake it anyway. Sam offered to pick me up, and we went to the crime scene in his car. We got there half an hour into the new year.

We pulled up to a nice brownstone in a nice neighborhood; not the kind of place you expect to find homicide detectives. Sam and I stood out like dirty, dented metal garbage cans at an outdoor wedding. The couple that lived there seemed decent enough; she offered us coffee first thing. Good coffee, too. Wasted on guys like us, but we weren't complaining. Her hands shook a little as she poured. We took it black.

The husband put his hand on his wife's shoulder, being strong for her. Nice. He informed me that he told the uniforms the whole story already. I asked him to humor me and tell it to me, too.

"Well, sir," he said. Sir. I could get used to working this side of town. "We noticed the smell the day before yesterday, but it didn't get really bad until this morning. We thought it was a raccoon maybe, so we called animal control. They came out and looked in the chimney and told us to call the cops. The police, I mean."

"'Cops' is fine," I said. "Anything else?"

"Well... when they left, I looked up there. I had to, you know? Now, I wish I hadn't."

"What'd you see?"

"A hand. A human hand. Kind of grey though, like spoiled meat." His wife (No ring. Girlfriend?) gagged a little and looked away. It was not an attractive sound. He put his arm around her.

"Okay. Thanks. Why don't you stay here while we take a look?" I handed him my card, the one that just says Detective James Hatfield, Homicide and a phone number. I have some others I got made that say "Ninja Master" but I didn't think this was a good time for levity.

Sam and I walked into the living room; yeah... you could smell it in here, all right. I walked to the fireplace and stuck my head in. I too could see the hand. Looked like it was dead maybe a week. I got out my skinny flashlight and shined it up the chimney. I kind of knew what I was going to find, but I still didn't believe it.

"Sam, you gotta see this." Sam and I changed places, and he whistled low as he looked up.

"Shit."

"Yeah."

The crime scene guys bustled around, taking pictures and fingerprints and finally got around to ah, extracting the body. It was him all right, but nobody would say it out loud.

We all just stood around him for a minute, looking down at his grey face with its white beard. His red suit with white trim.

So, we all jumped about a mile when we heard a loud 'thud!' in the fireplace. My heart pounded, I looked. It was a big bag, a sack. And it was all lumpy like it was full of stuff.

Nobody made a move toward it. I made sure my rubber gloves were on nice and tight and I stepped over to the bag. Very carefully, I opened it at the top.

"I'll be damned," I said. "It's toys."

Later, we'd get the autopsy results. Coroner said time of death was December 25th, sometime between 11:00 and midnight. There were a lot of details about organ size and weight, tissue decay, etc., but the one thing I couldn't get past was the guy's age. The report said he appears to be a man in his mid-sixties, overweight but otherwise healthy; still had all his original teeth (no fillings or dental work of any kind; this meant no dental records); but, while he appeared sixty-ish, the report had a lot of language in it like 'morphological and histological changes to the bone' that went right over my head, but I got the gist. By looking at the guy's femur, the coroner figures he had to be a couple thousand years old. At least. Maybe several thousand.

Don't believe me if you don't want to. I hardly believe it myself. I'll tell you one thing though. Next year? Christmas is really gonna suck.

Obsessive Compulsive Soldier

They said there would be side effects, but they were wrong. It's only one. One side effect, but one is plenty, believe me. If it's bad enough, one side effect is more than enough.

When I volunteered for this, I had visions of being the next Captain America. Or Batman. The Punisher. Nick Fury from S.H.I.E.L.D. Super-strong, super-patriotic... you know: a superhero. And it worked, kind of. I am much stronger than most people. I can take an enormous amount of abuse. I already had extensive martial arts and gymnastic training, and now I can use that to astounding effect, doing things that you see in movies, only I don't need any cables. I can run nearly twenty miles an hour and keep it up most of the day. I'm immune to most poisons, I never get sick and I'm muscled up like a monster. I don't even have to work out anymore. I still do though, when I can, because I enjoy it. Awesome, right?

It would be, if I could actually use any of it. If I could get out of this damn room and go fight the bad guys. They say they're working on it, but they've been saying that a long time. Every time they do, I smile and say something like, "I know you are. We'll lick this thing. Keep trying." I'm a good soldier. I have faith in my superiors. Most of the time. Pretty much. It gets harder, though. My optimism has its limits. I might have to give up hope one of these days.

The U.S. military (I'm not permitted to divulge which branch) has been trying for decades to come up with a new kind of soldier. They've literally been watching movies and reading comic books and trying to duplicate the bad-ass heroes they see there. The villains too I suppose; some of the villains are cool as hell.

At first, like most scientists, they experimented on animals. From what I hear, they had some pretty horrific results. I understand they made judicious use of the incinerator. But, they had some successes eventually. So, they started looking for volunteers among the enlisted. They pitched it pretty well, and soldiers lined up around the base to do it. Honestly, it wasn't that hard to sell the idea of being a superhero to kids who were already learning to kill for their country. You feel a little bit like that already after combat training.

This was early on, and things didn't go too well. Most of the volunteers died. They were the lucky ones. They didn't use the incinerator for these guys, but I think for some of them, they kind of wish they could have. Instead, they held a lot of closed-coffin funerals with full honors.

After about twenty years of frustration and failure, the military scientists finally started getting positive results. They figured out how to make soldiers heal faster, how to maximize their bodies' potential, how to increase bone density and strengthen muscle fiber. They figured out how, with a mix of intensive training, physical conditioning, injections and exposure to certain chemicals, they could make us pretty damn close to superheroes. I have no idea what was in those shots, or what chemicals they used. It's classified. Naturally.

By the time I came along and volunteered, they had ironed out most of the kinks with the program. We were all pretty confident I would be the first real success story. And, you know what? I was.

Except for that one side effect.

I'm still a patriot. I still love my country, and am still willing, hell, eager to serve. If I could just get out of this room. If I could just get away from the damn tiles. Six white tiles for every black. The whole floor is covered. I have to move the bed to get them all. And, of course, I do. Every time.

I'm a real superhero. Insanely tough. I no longer need to eat. I only need a gallon of water once a week. I no longer need sleep. I don't seem to be aging either. I am a total bad-ass now and one of these days I'm gonna get out of this room and go take out the bad guys, protect my country. But, right now, I have to start again. I count the black ones first, and then the white. I know I've counted them all already, and I know how many there are (seven hundred and forty-six).

They tried to put me in a room with no features, no tiles. They thought it would help. I know they meant well, but I kind of lost it when I had nothing to count. I did a lot of damage to the facility, so they moved me back. Eventually, they'll figure out a way to help me. Eventually, I'll be on the front lines where I belong. I keep waiting. And counting. Again and again. Over and over. It's only been two years. I can wait.

KEN MACGREGOR

ARCTIC WOLF

Gavin celebrated his thirty-first birthday by fighting a polar bear. He hadn't planned it; just worked out that way. He could have thought of worse ways to celebrate turning 31. In fact, he couldn't think of too many better.

He was feeling festive, so he let the big white bear live.

Gavin had been a werewolf for twelve years now, and he had traveled the U.S. and Canada looking for something bigger, stronger and tougher than him. So far, nothing even came close. Certainly, quite a few things were bigger, but that didn't make a whole lot of difference. He was the best, and he wanted a challenge.

There were some good fights in there, to be sure: the sharks off the New Hampshire coast; that grizzly in the Great Plains; the wolverine in northern Ontario - that sonofabitch was *mean!* None of them had his strength, his ability to heal; none were as ferocious, though the wolverine came close.

The only time he was really challenged was when he came across another werewolf. But, even they didn't pose much of a threat. He healed faster than most of his kind, and he was stronger and more agile than almost all the ones he had fought. Smarter, too. That wasn't hard. There were some really dumb werewolves. It was embarrassing. Most of the time, he just had to tear out the other wolf's throat. That usually took the fight out of them.

The only werewolf he ever had serious trouble with was back in Detroit. That guy was huge, even in his human form. He was crazy, too. Didn't know when to quit. The fight lasted most of an hour. To put it in perspective, Gavin usually ended things in six or seven minutes, and that's when he was toying with them. Gavin finally had to tear the guy to pieces; he was so feral he forgot himself and ate some. That was a mistake. Werewolf meat always gave him indigestion. He wondered how long it took that guy to pull himself back together; had to be two, three days at least. He would have already been in Wisconsin by then, where he saw more cows than he knew existed. He hooked up with a dark-haired go-go dancer in Madison. That was nice.

He was headed north, mostly hiking, sometimes thumbing a ride, when a trucker would stop - cars never did. He was chasing a rumor. An Alaskan fishing village, barely big enough to show up on the local maps, was supposed to have a monster. A monster that was rising up out of the sea and killing the locals. A really big, really scary monster. There were out-of-focus pictures of it on the internet. The only reason the 'X-Files' nuts weren't flocking to see it was that nobody wanted to go where it was that cold and where it was night for half the year. Gavin was headed there, though. Cold didn't bother him, and night was when he felt most alive. If this monster was for real, Gavin was going to fight it.

This was how he ended up fighting a polar bear, up in the part of Alaska that was the American equivalent of Siberia. Not much game around - not much anything - but, Gavin had wolfed out and nabbed himself a young seal; he was eating it on the ice when he got challenged by the big, white bear. This thing was stronger than the grizzly. Almost as strong as Gavin. Faster than he expected, too; he got clipped by a heavy paw he never saw coming. And it was big, especially up on those hind legs. The seal's blood on the ice was soon mixed with the combatants'. The bear finally figured out it was outclassed and walked away. It *walked* away. Gavin watched it go as his wounds closed. He was impressed.

Gavin finished his meal, happier than he'd been in days. He continued toward the village in wolf form, because the fur was warm. Cold couldn't kill him, but there was no reason to be uncomfortable. He arrived in the village well after dark. It was dark here a lot.

The village was maybe a mile, mile and a half across, stretched out across the icy coast. Most houses had lights on and smoke in the chimneys, but quite a few did not. He used his nose to find one that had been empty for a while. On the step, he changed. In his human form, he went inside, built a fire, found some clothes that almost fit, and settled in to wait. Less than an hour later, the door opened and four armed men walked in. Gavin could smell the gunpowder, but no silver. They were not a threat.

"English?" one said.

"Please," said Gavin.

"Why are you in Gary's house?" It was the same one.

"It didn't look like Gary was using it. And, it's cold outside."

"Where you from?"

"Brooklyn. New York."

"I know where Brooklyn is." He sneered. "We even have internet out here, man."

"Really?"

"Yeah, but we mostly use it to watch porn." He smiled. Gavin smiled back. Just a bunch of guys hanging out.

Everybody was still tense, though. Probably because they had guns and Gavin was a killing machine.

"No offense, buddy. There's a Brooklyn, Michigan. I think some other places, too."

"Okay. But why are you here, mysterious guy from Brooklyn? And how did you get here? No boats came today, there are no sled tracks out there. Only wolf tracks. Big ones. They come right up to the house here. That makes us wonder. It really does."

"Well," said Gavin. "You got me, Detective. I'm a werewolf." Three of the men flinched back, but the talker stood his ground.

"No shit?"

"No shit."

"What do you want with us?"

"Nothing. I don't kill humans. Not if I can help it."

"Why are you here, then?"

"For the monster. It's real, isn't it?"

"It's real. Gary, the guy's house you're in was eaten by the damn thing. So was my son. And nine other people. It comes out of the sea and grabs whoever's closest to the water, or if you're fishing, it comes up from below the kayak and rider and gulps them both down."

"Jesus. It must be huge!" He was getting pumped.

"Yeah. It is. You want to fight it? Fine. If you win, we can fish in peace again. If you lose, one less werewolf in the world."

"I've never lost."

"Always a first time."

"You got a name, tough guy?"

"Steve," said the talker.

"Gary and Steve. Nice Eskimo names."

"Fuck you."

"Guess I earned that. My name's Gavin. I don't want trouble."

"All right," said Steve. "But, the first time someone gets mauled, I'm breaking out the good silver."

"Not gonna happen. I'm gonna kill that thing and be on my way."

"Good luck, nook," one of the others said. "You're gonna need it."

"'Nook?'"

"Means 'white man'," said Steve. "From 'nanook', meaning 'polar bear'. 'Cause polar bears are white. Eskimo slang."

"Huh," Gavin said. "Learn something new every day."

***

Gavin worked with the villagers, staying human and doing all the nasty, dirty stuff no one else wanted to do; in a fishing village, this got pretty ugly. He worked for food; they let him stay in Gary's old house, since no one was using it anyway. Most of the people in the village didn't talk to him, but he wasn't bothered by it. They thought he was strange and dangerous; of course, they were right. He and Steve got along pretty well, for the most part. Gavin also got along with one other guy, named Bill. Bill was kind of slow. Not dumb or anything, but he seemed to take forever to process information and even longer to respond. He never complained about anything, so he ended up doing a lot of the shit work in the village, and Gavin did it with him.

He was there for five days before he finally got a glimpse of what he came for.

He was helping Bill strip blubber and meat from a seal; Gavin's job was to hold it still while Bill worked with a sharp, round blade. Gavin's mind was wandering. First, he thought about the seal he had killed, and how surprisingly tasty it was. He started to salivate and shook his head to clear it. He needed to stay human; he didn't want to scare Bill. Digging for something else to focus on, he thought back to a documentary he'd seen on almost exactly the same thing he was doing now. He tried to remember if it was on the Discovery Channel or if it was a video he'd checked out of the library. It was pre-wolf, he was sure of that. An Eskimo on that show used the same round knife, in the same way Bill did. That guy had no teeth; he was hooked on chocolate bars.

About fifty feet away, another guy whose name Gavin didn't know was pulling his kayak out of the water. He'd been fishing, and had a good haul. Gavin had seen this guy before; he always had a good haul. He was also one of the few people in the village who dared go out on a boat. Gavin wondered if was brave, stupid, or maybe both.

The man had just pulled his catch out of the kayak, when a giant head broke the surface; it was bigger than the house Gavin was staying in. It looked a bit like a lizard, one of the ones with long spikes radiating out and back from its neck, but it had rows of enormous, sharp-looking teeth like a shark. It continued to come out of the water, fifty or sixty feet of it rose in the air. Gavin wondered how much more of it there was.

"Sonofabitch," he said. "It's a dragon." Gavin was momentarily stunned; he just stood there, looking up at it. He recovered and kicked off his boots. Never taking his eyes off the dragon, Gavin pulled off his coat, too.

The fisherman turned to run, but the monster struck, cobra-fast and snagged him before he had taken five steps; the beast took up chunks of ice from underneath the Eskimo, too. As soon as that guy was gone, its massive head swiveled toward Gavin and Bill. Bill pulled his pistol fast, like a gunslinger and shot it three times. That was cool, but didn't seem to affect the dragon at all. Gavin calmly kicked off his new boots, took off his coat and looked at Bill. Bill looked back. The monster watched them both.

"You might want to run." Bill nodded. "Like, now, Bill." Bill ran. The monster followed his movements with his eyes, keeping his head pointed at Gavin. Gavin took off his shirt and dropped it on his coat and boots. Gavin stepped out of his pants, and stood naked in the cold. The beast gave him its full attention, curious. Gavin grinned at it.

"Let's dance," he said. He changed. He leaped.

This thing was fast. Gavin had to give it that. He was almost at its throat when it whipped around, dove forward and caught him in its mouth. The huge teeth severed his right foreleg at the knee: the leg that is his right arm in human form. Gavin mentally sighed. Why do sea creatures always have to eat his right arm? On the plus side, he didn't get bitten in half.

The dragon's considerable throat muscles were trying to pull him down, but he was not going easily. He dug in with his claws, knowing it had to hurt. He clamped his jaws down on a uvula the size of his own head and refused to let go. He hung there, blood dripping into his mouth, lending him strength, and watched his limb regrow. *I love being a werewolf*, he thought when he was whole again. He bit harder. The beast made a noise, almost a whimper. A very loud whimper. It thrashed back and forth, trying to dislodge this irritating thing that refused to be swallowed. It seemed to realize it couldn't and it stopped.

Gavin cocked an ear toward its teeth, wondering what it would do. He kicked his back legs hard, claws raking tender red flesh, figuring he might as well do some damage while he waited. Suddenly, the beast was moving again.

Then the mouth opened and sea water flooded in. *Ah*, thought Gavin taking a deep breath before the water engulfed him, *that was smart*. He had to let go to get enough air, and he got swallowed. Still, he used his claws all the down.

***

Steve and Bill stood with the other villagers and looked at the spot where the monster had gone under.

"You know," Bill said. "I was starting to like that guy."

"Issotoq?" Steve asked.

"No," said Bill after several seconds. "Gavin. Issotoq, too; that's a given."

Steve nodded, along with some others. They looked out at the sea.

"I was actually thinking he might have a chance," Bill continued. Steve nodded again. "Maybe he still does."

"No, Bill," Steve said. "He's a dead man."

Bill nodded. Everyone got back to work. Life was hard out here. There wasn't much room for sentiment.

***

Gavin shot out of the dragon's esophagus into a cavernous and stinking organ that had to be its stomach. He fell thirty feet onto large chunks of meat, bones, cartilage and whole fish which were everywhere in here. To his left was a village fisherman; likely the one he had just seen get eaten. That guy was still alive, but not for long, Gavin thought. He crawled across the body parts to check on him. The guy opened his eyes and panicked, yelling in a language Gavin couldn't understand. For a moment, Gavin was surprised and confused. Then, he remembered he was still a wolf and quickly changed.

"Sorry," he said. "Sorry! Sorry. Didn't mean to scare you."

"You are a werewolf," the guy said in English this time. "I didn't really believe you."

"Yeah. I get that a lot."

"Did we," he asked, "get eaten?"

"Yeah. But, I have a plan."

"Really?"

"Yeah. But, it's kind of crazy. I'm going to turn back into a wolf, rip a hole in the stomach lining and claw my way back up to its brain, maybe eating some of the heart and lungs on my way. Keep my strength up, you know?"

The other guy gagged.

"Oh," Gavin said. "Yeah. You're right. That's disgusting, isn't it?"

"What about me? What should I do?" Gavin looked at him for a long time.

"Stay alive, if you can. If I can pull this off, I'll come back for you."

"Why would you do that? You're a werewolf."

"Doesn't mean I'm a dick."

"Point. No offense meant."

"None taken." He put out his hand. "Maybe I'll see ya."

"I certainly hope so," he said, shaking Gavin's hand. "It's Gavin, right?"

"How'd you know?"

"Small village."

"Right."

"I'm Issotoq; it's Inuit; means God of Justice and Punishment."

"Finally," Gavin said, grinning. "A real god damn Eskimo." He clapped Issotoq on the shoulder with his other hand. "Let's see if we can't dole out some justice and punishment."

***

Issotoq was well-liked in the village. He kept the old ways alive and strong; he practiced shamanism and was one hell of a fisherman. He was also just a really nice guy, always willing to lend a hand and always generous with his catch.

The village held a feast to celebrate his life; they shared their stories of him and told his favorite jokes. The one about the drunken walrus got a huge laugh; it always did. They drank homemade beer and cracked a bottle of Russian vodka; they kept a case of it for special occasions. They were putting on a brave face, but they were all tired of losing good people.

As an afterthought, Steve and Bill said some nice things about Gavin, too. He'd been around for less than a week, so they didn't have a whole lot to say. There was mixed, if mostly positive reaction to that, and they all drank to the werewolf.

***

Gavin was a wolf again. He was eating really well today. He was ripping through muscle tissue as wide as a city street, tearing open arteries thick as those underwater cables. He had been holding his breath for about ten minutes now, and it was starting to hurt, but he knew relief was close. Closer than he thought, as the wolf abruptly tore through the lining of the dragon's lung and gulped in the air stored there. It occurred to him that he was lucky this thing didn't breathe with gills. He rested for a minute, taking huge, gulping breaths and thought about what he was going to do next. He wondered how the dragon was feeling with all the internal damage the wolf was causing. Maybe it hadn't even noticed. He shook himself, spraying blood from his fur all over the place. It was interesting, being inside something this big. It was like that old Raquel Welch movie where they travel around inside a guy's body in a little ship: "Fantastic Voyage" or "Fantastic Journey." Something like that. That was something else he'd seen in his pre-wolf days. Not much movie watching since he changed. As he sat in the giant lung, listening to air whistle out of the hole he'd made, he resolved to go see more. In the theater. That's the best way to see movies, he thought. If he made it out of here alive. Big if.

When he had recovered his strength, Gavin took a big breath, held it, and tore through yet another part of the lung, heading toward where he figured the heart would be. He would grab a quick bite of that on his way to the brain. This was fun! Gross, but fun.

He poked around for a while in the chest cavity, but he never did find the heart. Maybe dragons didn't have one. After several minutes, he saw light, and headed toward it. When he got there, he looked around and figured this was probably the ear canal. He approached the thing that looked like it might be the eardrum and he growled next to it, hoping to sound threatening, wondering if the dragon could hear him. Then, having satisfied his sense of the dramatic, he tried to push through the thick membrane separating him from the outside. It was really tough, and he had to use his claws to tear it first. When he ripped it open, the whole body jerked skyward and the beast bellowed. Oho! That hurt. Good. Serves you right for eating me, you giant freaking reptile, Gavin thought. He sat there in the dragon's ruptured ear, breathing in the sweet outside air. It was so much better and cleaner than the air in the lungs. The beast was staying above the water's surface now, possibly to keep water out of its damaged ear. Works for me, Gavin thought. He took one more deep breath and turned around.

***

Issotoq was not doing well. He couldn't feel his left foot, but he could feel most of the rest of him, and it hurt. He'd been making an effort to stay out of the digestive juices, but they were all over everything and it wasn't easy. Also, it was getting hard to breathe. The air, such as it was in there was foul, stinking and thick with carbon dioxide. Whatever oxygen the dragon had swallowed along with him was not going to last much longer. *Well*, he thought, *it has been a good life. Up until getting eaten by a monster anyway.* He smiled at the thought.

"That," he said aloud, "is an excellent epitaph."

***

Gavin followed the ear canal inward, thinking it must lead to the brain. He was right. Turns out a dragon's brain was big and light gray and convoluted; it looked a lot like a human brain. Only it was the size of a Hummer. Gavin grinned a crazy wolf grin and started in on it. He tore huge chunks out of the gray matter with his teeth and claws; he ate some, too.

132

It tasted like sushi. Not great sushi, but not the worst he'd ever had.

Gavin could feel the dragon moving, though the sense of motion was muted, distorted inside its head. Plus, he himself was moving, rending, tearing, eating; it was all kind of disorienting. He kept shredding his way through the brain, mentally singing a tune that had been stuck in his head for most of the day. He couldn't remember most of the words, just the chorus; his mind played the same words over and over. He hated that.

The sense of moving stopped. So he did, too. He cocked his ears, but could hear nothing.

He made his way along the ear canal again; it was easier this time, as the light poured in through the hole he'd punched in the membrane. Gavin was glad the sun was still up. He pushed his snout through the hole and sniffed, smelling only sea, then he put out his whole head. Finally, he climbed all the way out, squeezing his body through the hole. He crossed the massive cheekbone and stood on the dragon's snout, the whole beast floating on the surface of the icy sea.

It was dead. Most things are once you destroy their brain. He had won. For a long moment, he just stood on all fours and breathed. Then, he jumped in the water to wash off all the nasty stuff in his fur. He climbed back onto the snout, shook the water off with great enthusiasm; he changed into a man and stood, naked and triumphant. He pumped his fist into the air.

"Yes!" He looked around him at the empty sea. "I killed a *dragon!*" He spread his arms out and held for the applause. There wasn't any, of course. He stared out at the vast ocean. There was no land, not even any ice. He had no idea where he was. He let his arms fall to his sides.

"Well, shit."

***

Steve kissed his wife goodnight. Muriel had tears on her face, as she did every night since they had lost James. He held her and told her he loved her. He said they'd make it somehow. These were his words every night. He was always strong for her, and she loved him for it. Finally, she fell asleep and Steve stared at the ceiling in the dark room. When he was sure she was not going to wake up, he wept for his son. He did this every night, too.

***

Robert had been serving on the Persephone for two years. It was mostly dull, but had moments of excitement. Once, he saw a sperm whale breach completely out of the water. It couldn't have been more than two hundred yards from the boat. That was amazing. Things had been slow the last week, so everyone on the ship was doing busy work to keep from going stir-crazy. Robert was way up on the main mast, scrubbing bird shit off the pulleys, when he saw something really big. At first, he thought it was a Russian sub, and he was pumped. He was also really glad the cold war was over. He climbed down the mast and found Captain Lindsey.

The captain climbed to the roof of the topmost deck and looked out with his binoculars. When the captain saw it, he told his crew to drop everything and head that way. His was a research vessel, doing routine arctic exploration. They had been measuring glacial melt, important, but not glamorous. This, however was going to be huge! They were all going to be rich.

"Is it a sub?" Robert echoed his Captain's excitement.

"No, son. It's way better than that. You're about to be part of history."

The ship took about twenty minutes to reach the large object, and Robert couldn't believe his eyes. It was a genuine sea monster, and it was at least half again as long as the ship he was standing on. The whole crew gathered at the rail, making the ship list a bit starboard. They coasted along next to the beast, from the tail to its head. No one spoke.

***

Bill sat alone in his house. The fire in the pot-belly stove cracked and warmed the room. An iron pot of water sat on it, creating steam. Bill had sinus problems, and it helped. His hands worked carving a walrus tusk. It was a piece he'd been working on for years, whenever he had a quiet moment. Someday, it would be a mermaid. Right now, it looked more like a seal. Bill was a patient man, though. He'd get there eventually. He had originally started making it for the child he hoped to have. The boy or girl he hoped to have with Marybeth, but of course she was dead now. The dragon, or sea monster, or whatever it was had taken so much from them. From him. Bill felt the sadness of it like a heavy, wet blanket draped across his shoulders. He sighed, and resumed carving.

***

"Ahoy!" the monster said. The whole crew jumped, to a man.

"Ahoy!" the Captain called back. He was closest to the front, and had seen the naked man on the monster's snout. "Bit cold to be out here without your clothes, isn't it?"

"A bit," Gavin said. "But, I figured standing on a dragon's face in the middle of the ocean wasn't weird enough, so I decided to do it naked." Some of the crew laughed.

"Tell me that magnificent creature is alive!"

"Nope. It was, up until about half an hour ago."

"What happened to it?"

"I did."

There crew murmured amongst themselves, but nobody asked Gavin to clarify, so he didn't. Finally, the Captain found his voice.

"Would you like to come aboard, sir?"

"Very much, Captain. I was also wondering if you could give me a hand with something. A friend of mine is inside this thing, and may still be alive."

The crew lashed the dragon's body to the ship and set about opening its belly. This wasn't easy, as its hide was very hard to cut. Finally, they used a water cannon, setting it high as possible and creating an ultra-thin blast of water, slicing through the thing's scales. Once past that, they were able to cut through the softer tissue inside with ease. After a bit of searching, they found its stomach, and shortly after found Issotoq. He was alive, and quite surprised to be rescued.

"Where's Gavin?" he said. They told him he was getting cleaned up and dressed. "He's a good man. Do not fear him."

Using the limited medical facilities, the ship's doctor nursed Issotoq back to health, but she told him he'd need to go to a hospital, and that the tourniquet he had on now wasn't going to save that leg. Issotoq was pragmatic about it.

"Better a leg than a life," he said.

The Captain radioed in for a helicopter to take Issotoq to the closest ER and turned his attention to their other recent passenger. He was now wearing coveralls and a rain slicker someone had found for him. He was still barefoot, but didn't seem to mind.

"So," Captain Lindsey said. "You wanna tell me what happened out there?"

"Can you," asked Gavin, "think of any explanation that makes sense?"

"Nope. That's why I'm asking you."

"Fair enough. Let's just say I like to fight. I'm really good at it. I've never lost, and I've been having a really hard time finding an opponent good enough to challenge me."

"So, you took on a sea monster?"

"Yeah."

"And you won."

"Yeah. Wasn't easy, though."

"What? You let it eat you and fought your way out?"

"I wouldn't say 'let', but yeah, pretty much."

"You're not human."

"No. Not anymore."

"What the hell are you?"

"I'd rather not go there. I'm not a threat, not to you or your ship; let's leave it that, okay?"

"I guess we'll have to," the Captain said. "Can I drop you somewhere?"

Gavin gave him the name of the fishing village. They looked it up on the ship's computer.

"You have internet out here?"

"Yeah, but it's hell keeping the crew off the porn sites."

"Eskimos have the same problem," Gavin said.

***

The Persephone dropped anchor off the coast of the village. They loaded Gavin into a small boat with a couple of oarsmen and rowed to the icy shore. Steve was in front of the group of men who met them.

"Gavin," he said.

"Steve."

"I guess the world isn't short a werewolf."

"Not today anyway." Nobody spoke for a moment.

"Good."

Gavin smiled. Steve clapped him on the shoulder and smiled back. Then he frowned.

"Issotoq didn't make it?"

"He did, actually. Lost a leg, though. They took him to the hospital in a helicopter."

"Wow. The one Eskimo I can think of that wouldn't be impressed by a ride in a helicopter and he gets one. I'd give a limb to do that."

"So would he, apparently."

"I'll set 'em up, you knock 'em down."

Gavin grinned at him.

"Hey," Steve said, pointing out at the dragon. "You think we can eat that thing?"

"I had some. Wasn't bad. Problem is, these guys want to study it."

"Figures. Scientists. They probably won't even eat the meat or use the hide to make boats. What a waste. Anyway, I think we owe you big-time, friend."

"Nah," Gavin said. "That fight was the most fun I've ever had. It's why I came up here in the first place. You don't owe me a thing."

"Still," Steve said. "You want to stick around awhile, you know you're welcome."

"You guys get sharks out here?"

"Some. The Greenland Shark is almost as big as a Great White, but they're slow. Probably not much of a challenge for you."

"I really don't want to overstay my welcome..."

"We do have Killer Whales, though. Those guys are huge. Not sea monster huge, but, they're pretty fierce predators, I guess. And they're supposed to be almost as smart as us."

"Yeah? Okay. Maybe I'll stick around awhile."

"Good. Hungry? I got some chowder going at the house."

"Is it Manhattan style?"

"What the hell's the matter with you?"

"Kidding," Gavin held up his hands. "Where do you get the milk?"

"Sea Cows."

"Really?"

"No. We get a shipment every two weeks. Had you going, though."

On the way to Steve's house, Bill intercepted them. They looked at him, waiting, knowing he'd say what was on his mind eventually. But, he didn't say anything at all. Instead, he walked up to Gavin and embraced him, hugging him hard. He stepped back, nodded and walked away.

"Bill likes you," said Steve. Gavin nodded.

"Yeah. I like Bill, too." The two men went inside to eat. Gavin made Muriel laugh and she threatened to leave Steve for him.

"You can have her," Steve joked. It was a good night.

***

Three months later, Gavin was on the village computer; there was only the one. He was chasing a new rumor. Some people had been attacked by a giant, hairy biped in Nepal. They were calling it a yeti.

He grabbed the few things he had acquired here and brought them to Steve's house. When he handed them to him, Steve looked at him a long time, then nodded.

"You make sure you say goodbye to Bill before you go." Gavin nodded. "And, if you're ever in this part of the world again..." Gavin nodded again. "Don't get killed, all right?"

"I haven't yet," Gavin grinned.

"Always a first time." Steve grinned back. They embraced, clapped each other on the back and both wondered if they'd see each other again.

THE MONSTERS ARE REAL

"Do you believe in monsters?" Kelly was teasing him, Grant was sure. She did that a lot.

"No," he lied.

"I do," she said. Grant was sure she was just being contrary on purpose.

"Be quiet," he told his sister. "The babysitter will hear you."

"Who cares?"

"We're supposed to be asleep. She'll tell Dad."

"The T.V.'s on. She can't hear us."

They sat for a bit, listening to the T.V. downstairs. Grant tried to make out what the sitter was watching, but it was too muffled. He looked back at Kelly.

"You really believe in monsters?" He asked. She nodded. "So do I. I was lying before."

"I know. It's okay. It's a scary thing to admit." Grant nodded. It was.

Downstairs, the T.V. got a lot louder. They could hear car tires squealing and lots of gunfire.

"I guess she figures we're sleeping," Kelly said.

"Sounds like a cool movie," Grant said.

"Yeah. Must be nice to get paid to watch T.V." Kelly was bitter because her father didn't think she was old enough to be home alone with her little brother. She was *ten*, for god's sake! It was ridiculous. It didn't help that she didn't like the sitter. Helen, her name was. Who names their daughter Helen? Her parents must be cruel.

Kelly could tell as soon as Helen showed up that the teen girl didn't want to be there. She was probably missing a New Year's Eve party. Kelly was double-pissed because Helen wouldn't let them stay up to watch the ball drop on T.V.

Kelly hated to go to bed early, so she was taking it out on her seven-year-old brother. She gave him an evil grin.

"You know, Grant, you don't have to worry about monsters. They're afraid of Dad, so they won't come around."

"But," Grant said, "Dad's not home." His eyes grew wide.

"Oh yeah," Kelly said. "That might be a problem."

"Stop trying to scare me, Kelly."

"I'm just telling you the truth. You don't want me to lie, do you?"

Grant tried to decide whether it was worse to be lied to or scared. They seemed equally bad to him.

"Why are monsters afraid of Dad?"

"Because he's big," Kelly said, "and kind of scary sometimes." Grant thought about this.

"The sitter isn't as big as Dad. In fact, she's not much bigger than you."

"I know. She is kind of mean, though."

"I like her."

"You think she's pretty?"

"Ew. No. I think she's nice, though."

"Nice won't stop the monsters."

"Kelly!" Grant yelled at her. "Stop talking about monsters! You're scaring me." The T.V. noise stopped.

"Now you've done it," Kelly said. "She's going to tell Dad we stayed up late."

They strained their ears. They heard Helen's footsteps start up the stairs, then stop. They heard the front door, and Helen must have, too, because her steps went down again. Grant and Kelly both wondered if their Dad was home early. They could hear muffled voices downstairs: Helen's and a deeper voice. There was yelling.

Helen started screaming. It went on and on. There was a crash of something breaking, a loud thump, followed by six more thumps, and then silence. Kelly looked at Grant. Her eyes were huge. His, too. They looked at the bedroom door, but neither moved.

They heard the sound of feet on the stairs. Heavy feet, maybe wearing boots. Another sound followed the feet. A dragging, thumping noise. Kelly knew somehow that the second noise was Helen, being dragged up the steps.

"Kelly," whispered Grant. "Is it the monster?"

She nodded, afraid even to whisper.

"Is it going to get us?" Grant was shaking.

"Yes." He could barely hear her. The feet dragged their burden to the top of the stairs. They hesitated for a moment, then started down the hall toward the kids' rooms. Kelly and Grant were both in Grant's room. Kelly's room was between them and the stairs. They could hear the feet going in there. Kelly heard someone lie down on the squeaky springs of her bed.

Why would a monster lie down in my bed, she thought. Then she heard the feet again and understood. Helen was in her bed. She was bleeding and broken and dead, and she was in Kelly's bed. She made a small noise in her throat. The feet stopped outside Grant's door.

There was no lock.

The doorknob started to turn, clockwise. Kelly was sweating now. Grant's bladder let go, and the room filled with the smell of pee. Ignoring this, Kelly hugged her brother close.

"Please," she whispered. "Daddy, please come home now."

The door flew open and Kelly got her wish.

Sam Herringer, father to Kelly and Grant, widower of Victoria stood in the doorway. There was a shiny, wet tire iron in his hand and he was spattered all over with red. Sam looked at his kids, huddled together on the floor. He checked his watch.

"It's ten thirty. You're still up?"

"Sorry," Kelly said. Grant was too afraid to speak.

"Doesn't matter," Sam said. "You know what, guys? In four hours, it will be exactly one year since your mother was killed. One year since I drove home drunk from a party and slammed her side of the car into a lamppost. One year since the light went out of my life."

"Dad," Kelly said. "Did you stop taking your medicine?"

"Medicine? That's not medicine! It's poison! That damn shrink is trying to kill me."

Grant and Kelly said nothing. They were terrified. It didn't help being reminded of their Mom; they missed her even more than their Dad did. But, kids are more resilient than adults. Like trees, the young ones bend.

"Daddy?" With that one word, Grant pleaded for their lives.

"Oh, don't worry, little man," his Dad smiled at him, sending the tire iron clanging to the floor. He wiped his hands on his shirt. "This was just for the babysitter."

"Thank goodness!" Kelly let go of her brother and started toward her Dad. "For a minute, I thought you were going to..."

She stopped when her Dad pulled the pistol from the back of his belt.

"I always wondered what it was like to kill someone. On purpose, I mean." He laughed. It was like his usual laugh, only broken. "That's why I beat the babysitter to death with the tire iron. Wasn't easy. She put up quite a fight at first. Screamed a lot, too. You probably heard." They nodded, both staring at the gun. "But, for us, for *family*, we should be merciful. Right?"

"Right, Dad," Kelly managed. Grant nodded, trying to smile. He started to relax. Everything was going to be okay. Daddy was home. The monsters couldn't get them. Monsters were afraid of Dad.

Kelly knew better. Sometimes, the monsters looked like people. Sometimes, they stood right in front of you and you didn't know until it was too late.

"Right," Sam said. "Therefore, the gun. Quick and mostly painless. Who's first? Kelly? You're the oldest."

Without waiting for an answer, he shot his daughter in the head. She was dead instantly. Grant screamed and scuttled back to the wall. He screamed again, then stopped, staring at his Dad. That was weird. There was a red dot on his forehead. For a moment, Grant's father looked like his old self.

"What, Grant? Why are you looking at me like that?"

There was a muffled "thump", the window broke and Sam fell backward, a neat hole in his forehead. For several seconds nothing happened. Then, everything was chaos.

Cops filled the room, taking Grant away from the nightmare where his father and sister were missing the backs of their heads. In the hallway, passing Kelly's room, he caught a glimpse of the babysitter, Helen, on his sister's bed. Her eyes were open, and it seemed she looked at him as he went by. That image, even more than witnessing the violent deaths of his sister and father, haunted him for the rest of his life.

Bazooka Jim

Jim Baldwin was surrounded by potatoes and zombies. Thankfully, only the potatoes were in reach. Jim loaded his potato cannon with a fresh spud and looked over the edge of the flat roof. Three floors down, closer than he liked, was the shuffling horde. The undead below him stood in place, rocking from one foot the next, like people trying to stay warm on the train platform. Jim set the cannon on his shoulder, sighted down the barrel and picked his target: Ms. Harper, his seventh grade teacher. Jim had loved seventh grade. Ms. Harper was a teller of tales. She had traveled to Europe and Asia and New Zealand and taught the class practical and moral lessons using examples from abroad. She was one of those teachers you go back to visit as an adult. Now, Ms. Harper was a shambling, flesh-eating monster. Jim carefully lined up the crosshairs on her face and squeezed the trigger. A second later, Ms. Harper's head exploded and her legs gave out. The dead next to her paused and glanced down for a moment, then returned their focus to the roof, back to Jim. He reloaded.

Last summer, Brookline, Mass. was a nice, quiet New England town. Lots of old money lived there, but they still had rent control, so the population was a mixed bag. Jim had grown up in the closest thing Brookline had to seedy neighborhood. It was still a safe neighborhood, but they had roaches and the superintendent always smelled like beer and fish. His dad raised him alone; his mom took off when he was six. He saw her for two weeks in the summer and on Christmas every year. Jim loved his mom, because, well, you have to, right? He didn't much like her though, and saw his visits with her as a duty. Anyway, now Brookline was crawling with the walking dead, and it didn't matter a damn who had money, or who left whom behind. Jim picked his next target.

Max Taylor had been Jim's best friend since their freshman year. They used to ride the backs of the trains, standing on the coupler, holding onto the wipers, so they wouldn't have to pay. On Saturday nights, they drank Rolling Rock and sometimes did too much acid. They once smoked the most amazing weed they got from a 'Nam vet who somehow kept his connection over there. That was an epic high. Jim and Max were inseparable; even after they both fell for Gina Winter. They both dated her, both slept with her, but they got over it. They would be seniors now, class of '85, probably both trying to get the unattainable Katie Smith to go to the prom. Max used to introduce himself as Maximum Taylor, though his name was just Max, not short for anything.

Zombie Max had lost his left hand; when he was alive, he had been left-handed. Max was wearing the varsity jacket he earned running track. The big B over the breast was stained black with old blood. Jim stared at his old friend, looked into Max's sunken eyes, trying to see some spark of the boy he knew. Nothing. Jim fired, the carbon dioxide whoosh followed by the thump of the potato plowing through Max's forehead. Max's jaw dropped open, making him look surprised. Maybe he was; Max had helped Jim build that potato cannon. It took Max's body a moment to register that the top half of his brain was missing. When it did, it fell forward, toppling like a domino. Jim was pleased to see the potato decapitated the zombie behind Max, too. Lucky that guy was short or it would have been a chest shot.

"Two for one. Badass." Time for a break. The dead would wait. Jim stepped away from the edge and set the cannon down. He wanted to name his weapon, but hadn't thought of anything cool yet. Jim pawed through his huge red frame backpack looking for food. He had hundreds of potatoes, but they were raw, and besides, they were ammo. Jim's larder was still pretty well stocked, and he silently thanked himself for thinking ahead. When the whole thing started, Jim bought the backpack and stocked it. He filled his canteen and four one-gallon jugs with water. When everyone else evacuated his building, Jim locked the doors and went to the roof, locking the access door. Kinda scuzzy though it may be, this was his home, and he was going to defend it. Jim had the padlock key; if he ran low on supplies, he could forage in the empty apartments. It was the perfect set-up, Jim thought.

Jim grabbed a can of Chef Boyardee ravioli and cranked the can opener around the top. He ate it cold; the taste reminded him of being at his mom's. She used to feed Jim this stuff, barely warmed up in a saucepan. She couldn't be bothered to put much effort into lunch. Not for the first time, Jim pictured his mom down among the dead. It was a shitty thing to want, to put a high-velocity tuber through your zombie mom's head, but he couldn't help it.

The sound of breaking glass snapped him out of his reverie.

Jim looked over the edge nearest him, to the east. Nothing had changed there. Jim sped to the north edge, but it was the same: 50 or so milling bodies there, too. On the west side, things were bad. Somehow, maybe just by the press of bodies, the zombies had broken the glass doors of his building. Now, they were streaming in.

"Shit."

Jim ran to the roof access door to check the lock. He ran around the roof looking for heavy things to block it in case the lock failed. The pasta and meat made a leaden lump in Jim's gut as he loaded his cannon with a fresh potato. He would be 18 in three months. A man. It occurred to Jim that he had done a surprising amount of stupid shit in his short life on this planet. He'd done some good, too, of course. Like when Staci Peterson's dog died; Jim dug a grave in her yard, in the rain and read aloud to her from the book "Marley." Jim held her while she cried and laughed with her at the funny parts. And, not once did he make a move on her, though he did look down her shirt a couple times. Hey, he was fifteen. Staci always smiled at Jim after that, even when she was hanging out with her cool friends, and Jim was walking with the stoners and geeks. So, maybe he had been a decent guy after all, despite the beer and drugs and the low-level crime he and Max got into almost every month.

The door rattled. Jim still hadn't found anything to block it. All he had was a huge pile of potatoes. Somehow, Jim didn't think that was going to cut it. The door was held shut by a Yale padlock that was supposed to be able to take a bullet and stay locked. But the door itself was wood, and it looked old and cheap. Jim stood as far from it as the roof would allow and shouldered his cannon. He took deep, steady breaths trying to stay calm, but his heart was racing. David Bowie's "Panic in Detroit" was running through Jim's head. He didn't know any lyrics besides the chorus, so that played over and over. Behind and below him, Jim could hear the shuffle-shuffle sounds of the dead. Rock and a hard place, he thought. The door groaned, bulged outward and a crack appeared in the middle. Jim shifted his weight so he was balanced and ready. A second potato was in his jacket pocket, hundreds at his feet; he wondered if he'd have time to reload. The door gave.

The cheap wood split in two, half staying partly attached by the hinges. The side with the padlock fell all the way off, the steel lock skittering across the tar. The first two zombies fell through the gap face-first, and the ones behind stepped on them to get by. Jim fired, blowing a hole in the nearest one's head, taking off half the face of the one behind it. Another two for one. Jim swung the cannon down and slapped the second potato into the tube. He set it on his shoulder again and aimed at the closest corpse, now only about 20 feet away. This time, the spud caught it just above the top row of teeth, leaving a hole Jim could see through. The dead man dropped, and Jim saw his last projectile imbedded in the chest of the one behind him.

Jim squatted, grabbing another potato. As fast as he could, he slammed it home and brought the cannon up. There was a zombie inches from the other end. Jim's finger froze on the trigger. He couldn't move, even though he could see the other dead moving in on him from the sides.

"Hi, mom," Jim said. She hissed at him, lunging forward, mouth wide open. He fired. He got his wish. His mother's brain exploded behind her, riding a potato at high speed. Jim knew he had no chance. He ducked under a grasping claw-like hand, grabbed one more potato and leaped over the edge. As Jim fell, he loaded the cannon. Time stretched for Jim as he fell, and he named his cannon: MomSlayer. It would have to do. The zombies below crowded under him, hungry for his flesh. They broke his fall and Jim lived long enough to shoot Marcy Gilbert. He'd had a crush on her in seventh grade. Marcy sat two desks away in Ms. Harper's class, and Jim spent many hours mooning over her. Now, she was a zombie with a big hole where her face used to be. The last thing Jim thought before he was torn apart and eaten was that Marcy was still kind of pretty before he shot her, despite, you know, everything.

FIRST PERSON SHOOTER

Cain stands motionless, surveying the damage. He absently rubs the mark on his cheek; it has been there a long, long time, but he's not likely to forget the day he got it. Cain inhales through his nose; he has come to appreciate, even enjoy the sharp coppery smell of fresh blood. He lifts a foot, shakes some of it off the toe of his Italian loafer and steps back across the threshold. A job well done, he thinks, and drops the heavy cleaver on the floor. The blade thunks into the wood. As his footsteps fade, the flies begin to gather for the feast.

***

THIS IS INTOLERABLE.

"I know," Adam says. "But what can we do? No one can touch him; you made sure of that." He is careful to keep his tone respectful; he is stating a fact, not admonishing. One does not admonish Him.

THERE IS A LOOPHOLE.

"Really?" Adam arches a perfect eyebrow. "You never mentioned this before."

I DO NOT ENTIRELY TRUST YOU, YOU KNOW.

"Yes," Adam sighs. "I know. You hold a grudge better and longer than anyone."

I DO EVERYTHING BETTER AND LONGER THAN ANYONE.

Adam's eyebrow shoots up.

GET YOUR MIND OUT OF THE GUTTER.

Adam laughs, then gets serious.

"What loophole?"

THE MARK WILL ONLY AFFECT THOSE BORN AFTER CAIN. ANYONE OLDER THAN CAIN MAY DO HIM HARM WITHOUT CONSEQUENCE.

"Okay," Adam says. "But, there are only two people older than Cain."

PRECISELY.

Adam stares at his Creator for a long moment.

"You want me to kill my own son?"

ALL OF HUMANKIND ARE YOUR CHILDREN, ADAM.

"Technically, sure," Adam said, "but I wasn't their father. Not really. Not in a hands-on, kissing boo-boos, singing to sleep, teaching about the world way. Not in any way that counts."

YOU ARE THE ONLY ONE WHO CAN DO THIS.

"What about Eve?"

DO NOT SPEAK OF HER IN MY PRESENCE.

"I always forget how much you hate her."

I DO NOT HATE. I AM LOVE. STILL, YOU WILL REFRAIN FROM SAYING HER NAME. IT ANNOYS ME.

"Of course," Adam says. "Whatever you say. Since I seem to be the only choice, what would you have me do, exactly?"

YOU NEED TO PUT AN END TO IT. YOU NEED TO DO IT NOW.

Adam sighs. It's no use arguing with God. You never win.

**

Cain smiles at the cop in plainclothes, probably a detective, most likely homicide. The cop is holding the automatic steadily, pointing at Cain's center mass.

"Put your hands behind your head," he is saying. "This can go easy for you if you cooperate."

"And," Cain says, moving a step closer. "If I don't?"

"Then it will go hard," says the cop, undoing the safety. His legs shift to a shooting stance.

"Pull the trigger, officer." Another step.

"'Detective'." The cop is sweating. His gun hand shakes, just a little. "You're gonna want to stop walking now, sir."

"I don't think so," Cain says. "Detective. You go ahead and pull that trigger. I don't mind. It would really be a refreshing change of pace." Another step. The gun barrel is resting squarely against Cain's chest. The cop is wet with sweat now.

"What," he manages, "is that thing on your face?"

"My curse," Cain says. "And, as it turns out, yours, too." Cain gently takes the gun from the others hand; the cop is relieved to let it go. Cain turns it around, racks the slide, which is unnecessary but fun, and puts the barrel to the detective's forehead.

"Why?"

"To get His attention. It's nothing personal. Bye now." Cain pulls the trigger and the detective's last thoughts explode against the brick wall.

***

Adam knows it is a different world now; he checks in every couple hundred years. Heaven is perfect, of course, but he still gets nostalgic for his first home. Well, second home, he supposes. Knowing it's a different world doesn't prepare him for the noise. And the smells. And the dirt. And the mountain-high buildings. And the people. So many people! Adam feels an overwhelming sense of responsibility. Look what happened! He thinks. All of this, from me? Well, from God, of course, but through me. I have billions of children.

"Only, there's one I have to kill."

"Excuse me?" asks a woman at the newsstand, who is unable to hide how compelling she finds him.

"I am sad, because I have been tasked by God to kill my firstborn son."

She steps away from him, confused and afraid. She doesn't go far, though; she is unable to shake the feeling that she somehow knows this man. Somehow, that fact is important, significant.

"You understand I hope," Adam says. "I don't want to do it, but there is no one else."

A crowd is gathering; they all look at Adam the same way: is he famous? How do we know him? Who is this guy? They are drawn to him and the crowd gets bigger. When Adam walks, they follow; soon, there are dozens, then hundreds. It's an impromptu parade, stopping traffic and growing larger by the moment. Adam knows where he is going; he was put on Earth mere blocks from Cain's last victim. He is drawn to Cain; he can feel him close now.

***

Cain holds the young woman's head in his hands, gently. He looks into her eyes, strokes her cheek. A tear falls from her face; she intuits what is about to happen. Cain catches it with a finger and tastes it.

"Sh. Don't cry. You're quite pretty, you know? Yes. You are. So, I will leave your pretty face intact. Sadly, soon it will all be rot and bone and dust; beauty does not last, child. I learned that early on."

Cain jerks, feeling a presence, one he knows, one that shouldn't be here. He looks toward it and he can hear the tide-like click and swish of hundreds of pants and shoes. Cain knows now that he got the Big Guy's attention; he knows that steps are being taken to deal with the problem. It's about fucking time.

His hands are wet. He looks back at the woman and the carnage that is left of her head.

"Damn it. Look what you made me do," he mumbles, and wipes his hands on his shirt. He goes to meet his father.

***

Adam and Cain look at each other for the first time in millennia. The crowd, well over a thousand strong, spreads out, framing them on the wide street.

"You look good," Adam says.

"You too."

"Why?" Adam asks.

"How about revenge?" Cain returns. "I did suffer for eons in the Land of Nod; you have no idea how unspeakably dull that was. And, when they finally let me out, I spent another eternity wandering the Earth, condemned to live forever with this lovely parting gift on my face. So, I know you're here to reason with me, to talk me down, but it's not gonna happen... Dad."

"That's not why I'm here," says Adam, pulling out a large caliber automatic. "I'm here to end this."

"Oh," Cain laughs. "This should be interesting." He leaps the thirty feet separating them, drawing a carving knife from his belt. The crowd gasps. It is graceful and terrifying, but Adam calmly puts five bullets in Cain's chest before he's halfway there. Momentum carries him nearly to Adam's feet.

"Ow," Says Cain, looking up from the ground. "Where did you learn to shoot?"

"Lethal Weapon movies."

"They have those up there?"

"Of course. It's Heaven." Adam smiles at his bleeding son.

"You turned out to be a pretty good father" Cain says, teeth clenched.

"What makes you say that?"

"I just wanted to die." Cain says. "I'm so damn tired."

"I know," Adam says.

"Will I see you again?"

"Yeah. Eventually. You'll go down first," Adam says. Cain's eyes slide shut, then snap open again.

"Not much time left, I'm afraid." Cain says. "Would have been nice to talk. To catch up a little."

"Some other time," Adam says.

"Count on it."

"Cain?"

"Yeah?"

"Say hi to your mother for me."

Cain nods, coughs once and dies.

***

Adam stays long enough to smooth things over with the locals. It's easy, as the bullet-ridden body is the serial killer the police have been, sometimes literally, dying to catch. Also, because he's the First Father, and everyone wants to trust him. Then, having done the right thing, the hard thing, Adam goes home. The other home. The pretty, quiet one.

He tosses the pistol at God's feet and tells him it's done. Adam knows this gesture is pointless, that God already knows, but he does it anyway. The drama appeals to him.

KAREN GETS HER MAN

Karen squatted inside the chalk circle, ready to spring. She gripped the ceremonial dagger in her right hand. More than once, doing this sort of thing, she had needed it. Karen could feel the heat from the five big, white candles on her skin, the flames licking improbably high. Karen was naked; once years ago, her robe had caught fire, and she was not going to go through that again.

Besides, she wanted to make a good first impression. Karen said the final words of the spell and felt power flow into her from the floor, through the balls of her feet and all the way to her head. Karen grinned. She loved this part. She held the energy as long as she could stand it. Finally, Karen opened her mouth, vomiting forth a Word of Power.

Just outside the circle, the air ripped open. A dimensional rent, wider in the middle, tapering at the top and bottom. It looks like a vagina, Karen thought. She could see movement through the rift, but couldn't focus on it. Her eyes kept slipping away, her mind refusing to grasp what was there. Karen turned her head, and watched from the corner of her eye. She stood, knees creaking, and held the blade ready, just in case.

There he is, Karen thought. Martin's head pushed through the crack first, hair matted with filth and blood. Martin pushed an arm out into the real world, and slapped the floor with his palm. One shoulder was free now, and Martin dragged his other arm out. He twisted his body so it was face-down; it looked like he was going to do push-ups. Martin lifted his face, tendons in his neck straining. His eyes were still closed. Karen watched, rapt, as her former lover came back. Inch by inch, his naked body emerged from the Interdimensional Birth Canal. As Martin pulled his first foot through, the hole collapsed around his other leg, holding his foot on the other side. Martin opened his eyes and saw Karen. He reached for her, pleading. Karen kept her expression neutral, waiting to see what would happen. Martin looked back at his trapped foot. He flipped onto his back and grabbed his stuck leg. Martin pulled hard, shoulder and arm muscles bunching. Karen admired the play of strength under Martin's filthy skin. He had always been nice to look at. If he makes it, the first thing we do is get him in the shower, she thought. Martin struggled and strained and was finally rewarded; his foot came free with a pop and the hole was gone.

Karen watched Martin. He looked like himself, but she was not one to take chances. For several seconds, Martin just lay on the basement floor, breathing hard, eyes once again closed. He tilted his head back and looked at her.

"Karen," he rasped. She nodded. Martin rolled over, pulled his knees under him and stood up, not quite steady on his feet. He took in the chalk circle, the candles, and the naked woman in the middle. Karen. His wife.

"You brought me back," Martin said. "You brought me back from… there."

"Come here," Karen said. She opened her arms, welcoming him. The dagger was folded back against her forearm, invisible. For a moment, Martin hesitated, but he walked toward her. Karen watched his feet as they broke the chalk circle, confirming he was human. Then, he was in her arms. She held him tight, ignoring the reek of offal in her nose. She felt him getting aroused, and backed away. Martin never even noticed the knife.

"Let's get you into the shower," she said.

"How did you do it?" Martin asked. "Not that I'm complaining. I'm very happy to be back. Very, very happy." He eyed her naked body in a proprietary way.

"I'm a witch," Karen said. "You knew that."

"Okay," Martin said. "Don't tell me how. I'm just glad you did. I really hated that place."

Martin stating the obvious again. Karen had always disliked that about him. But, she smiled at him. That really was the least of his faults.

"I know," she told him. "But, you're back now, and you'll never have to go there again."

"Do you have anything to eat? I haven't had food in ages." He stretched, yawned and scratched his crotch. Karen flashed him a dazzling smile as if she did not find him repulsive.

"Shower first. Please."

Karen gestured for him to head upstairs. When he went, she wiped off the muck from her skin with a towel and put on a robe. She went up the stairs and listened to the shower running through the open bathroom door. Karen hoped that the gunk he was washing off didn't clog her drain. Might be hard to explain what it was to a plumber.

Karen heard the shower shut off from the kitchen. She made a green pepper and cheddar omelet with four eggs. She seasoned it with salt, pepper, a dash of garlic and oregano and just a hint of ginger. It was a textbook flip. Karen cut it in half and slid it onto two plates. She poured fresh-squeezed O.J.

into short glasses and set out forks as Martin walked in. He was wearing the pajama bottoms Karen had set out for him, but not the top. He really did have a nice body, she thought. Pity about the rest of him. He dropped into the chair and devoured the omelet.

"Mm," Martin said. "Thanks, babe. That hit the spot."

"I'm glad you liked it," Karen said.

"I've missed this," Martin said. "Not just you making me breakfast. I mean, I missed you. I missed your face."

Not every time, Karen thought. Sometimes your aim was spot on. But she smiled at Martin, keeping her thoughts to herself.

"I missed you, too, honey. I worked very hard to get you back, and I am very happy to see you."

"You know what else I missed?" Martin leered at her.

"I think I can guess."

"I'm nice and clean now, baby. We got a lot of lost time to make up for."

"Martin," Karen said. "Give me a chance to get used to the idea of having you back, okay? We have plenty of time."

Martin did not look happy, but he nodded. Karen cleared the dishes from the table. She heard him push his chair back and glanced into the dining room. Martin was looking at a picture on the wall. It was from happier times, early in their marriage, before she knew what he was. In the shot were their friends Gina and Tom. That picture was taken on Cape Cod.

"Remember this summer?" Martin asked.

"Mm-hmm."

"You ever hear from Tom and Gina anymore?"

"No."

"I wonder how they are," Martin said. Karen waited.

"You know," Martin continued. "Gina wanted to do me. Showed me her tits and everything." He watched Karen's face to see how she'd react.

"Oh? She never told me that."

"She had perfect tits. I can still picture them. I always thought we should invite her into our bed. I would love to have both of you at once."

Martin sidled up to her, cupped her ass with his hand, squeezed hard. Too hard. It hurt. He was back, all right. Martin pulled his hand back like it had been shocked.

"Ow," Martin said, rubbing his hand. "Cramped up on me there."

"Martin," Karen said. "I left the garbage cans at the curb. Would you mind going to get them for me?"

"No problem," Martin said.

Karen smiled and watched him go to the front door and open it. Outside, the morning sun was twinkling off the dew covered trees. He took a step outside and was blown back five feet. He sat for a moment, staring at the open doorway. Then, Martin turned to Karen, comprehension crawling across his face.

"You bitch," he spat. "You fucking bitch. Why bring me back at all then?"

"Because, Martin. After the way you treated me, Hell is not punishment enough for you."

"I should have nailed Gina when I had the chance," Martin said.

"Instead of three months later?" Karen asked. "I know about everything, Martin. I'm a witch, remember?"

Martin ran at her, fists up to smash her face. Karen could almost smell his rage. She stood her ground. When Martin was just inches away, he screamed in agony and fell to his knees.

"You didn't think I'd let you hurt me, did you? Every time you try to harm me, or try to leave, the pain will be worse. But, it will never kill you, Martin. No. You're going to be around for a long, long time, and I'm going to thoroughly enjoy making you pay."

"How? What are you going to do to me?"

"I thought I'd start with this." Karen kicked Martin in the balls as hard as she could. He went down, holding himself. Karen could hear him sobbing quietly.

"I'm sorry," Martin said. "I am so sorry for being cruel. For hitting you. For cheating on you. You have no idea how sorry I am." Martin sounded contrite.

She almost believed him.

"No. You're right," Karen said. "I don't. But, I know how sorry you will be."

LAWN

The old man across the street was watering his lawn again; he did it every single day. The old man used a yellow trigger on the end of a green hose; the trigger made Harvey think of a gun. Harvey's dad said the old man was wasting an unconscionable amount of water, though that he had to admit it was a damn fine-looking lawn. Harvey had to admit it, too, though he wasn't sure what unconscionable meant, and he wasn't allowed to say damn. The old man's lawn was a deep, rich green, and it looked soft like the expensive plush carpet at Uncle Kyle's enormous house. Kyle wasn't really an uncle; he was a family friend, but Harvey's parents always called him Uncle Kyle. He was what Harvey's family called well-off. Once, when visiting them, Uncle Kyle took Harvey and his family out to lunch at his hotel. Harvey didn't remember what he ate, but he never forgot Uncle Kyle putting down two hundred dollar bills to pay the tab. For lunch. For four people. Wow.

The old man always glared at the neighborhood kids from his porch if they came near. Harvey and his friends were afraid of him. It really was a perfect lawn. Maybe the weeds were scared, too.

Ornate printed signs stood sentry at each corner of the old man's lawn: Keep Off the Grass. If the old man caught you so much as leaning over his lawn, he'd be out on his porch, fast as a cat, snarling and growling at you, spittle and unintelligible syllables flying out of his mouth.

The old man frightened Harvey more than his friends. Maybe it was because he lived right across the street, so Harvey saw him every day. Four teeth remained in that ancient maw; skin and clothes hung loose on his scarecrow bones; his crumpled gray-brown face worn down by time. The only thing with any semblance of vitality on the old man were his eyes. The same green as the lawn, and sharp, those eyes, like a raptor. Harvey imagined the old man as a vulture, wicked hook of a beak snapping open and shut, talons gripping a stone outcropping, dirty feathers rustling over old, thin bones. The old bird would wait, patient as the tomb, for the deadly sun to kill a small, thirsty boy. Then, the wings would spread wide and the foul creature would spiral down to the hot rocky ground and pick at the poor boy's carcass. Harvey imagined that, even though he was already dead, he would feel the tug as the ancient vulture plucked out his eye.

Harvey looked up to find the old man gazing at him, the hose in his hand forgotten. For a long time, their eyes remained locked. The old man grinned, showing his few teeth and nodded, breaking their eye contact and watering his perfect lawn. Harvey shook it off and went inside and straight to his room. He had homework; he might as well get it over with.

From his window, Harvey could see the old man's house. The old man wasn't out front now; the hose was coiled neatly by the front steps. The rich, green lawn waved back and forth and Harvey looked up. He liked to watch the leaves blow in the breeze. The leaves were still. There was no wind. Harvey looked back at the lawn. It was still moving.

Homework forgotten, Harvey sidled into the hall, listening. He could hear the TV downstairs, so Dad occupied; he had no idea where Mom was. Harvey tiptoed down the stairs looking out for Mom the whole time. When he didn't see her, he knew she must either be in the basement or the backyard. Either way, Harvey was in the clear. He didn't want to have to explain to his parents about the moving lawn. He opened the front door, grateful that the hinges didn't squeal and stepped outside. As he crossed the street, looking both ways, it occurred to Harvey that doing this sort of thing in broad daylight wasn't what the hero in a book would do, but it seemed a heck of a lot safer than night. Plus, though he would deny it if asked, Harvey, at eleven, was still kind of scared of the dark.

When Harvey set foot on the opposite curb, he noticed the lawn was still swaying. He stepped to the sidewalk's edge, inches from the lush, green blades and they stopped. Harvey swallowed hard, staying as still as he could. After several seconds of no change, Harvey gathered his courage and strode up the walk to the old man's porch. Just before the steps lay the garden hose, yellow snake head nestled atop the skinny green body. Harvey picked up the handle. It wasn't as heavy as he expected. Squatting at the edge of the lawn, Harvey reached out with the hose handle, the green rubber hose scraping on the cement as it unwound a little. Harvey poked the lawn.

The grass grew before his eyes. In an area roughly a foot wide, the lawn was instantly two feet long. The blades curled around the yellow gun, his fingers, hand and wrist, and they were strong.

"Leggo," Harvey yelled. "Leggo, leggo, damn you!" He pulled back as hard as he could, but the grass wouldn't break. Harvey couldn't uproot it. It wouldn't let go. It pulled him toward itself. It was an eager tug. Harvey planted his feet and leaned back. He screamed, not caring if he sounded like a scared little kid.

Suddenly, he was free. Harvey fell back on his tailbone, bruising it. He wouldn't sit well for four days. The long grass still clung to his hand and wrist, still pinned the yellow gun to his hand, but it no longer tugged. It no longer moved. He looked up. The old man stood there, holding a long curved blade; it was the kind Harvey had seen on the DVD covers of more than one horror movie. The blade was stained with green liquid; it was the same color as the grass, as the old man's eyes. Harvey stared at the blade. The grass bleeds, he thought. The old man helped Harvey to his feet. Harvey could smell coffee and peppermint on the old man's breath. The old man marched Harvey by the shoulders to the sidewalk, where Harvey stammered his thanks. The old man stared at him for several seconds, saying nothing. Finally, the old man spoke.

"Keep off the grass."

Deadweight

Gregory Simmons was virtually awesome. Not so much in the real world, but his Avatar was: tall, handsome and grotesquely muscular; he could run and leap and fight and even fuck, if you knew the cheat codes. Gregory Simmons did, but he only used that particular cheat one time, just to see; it was awkward, like walking in on your brother and his girlfriend. Other than satisfying his curiosity, though, he refused to use cheat codes. If you win without playing the game by the rules, what's the point? And Gregory Simmons was going to win. So far, he'd won every game he ever played. It was only a matter of time until be beat this one.

He was playing "Gods of Kromm" now. His Avatar, Blackstone, had leveled up as high as he could go, but there were still four challenges he had yet to complete. Gregory made Blackstone jump up and down a few times and flex his biceps. A farm girl on the screen swooned; it was a nice touch. Gregory flipped screens to check vital stats; everything was perfect. His phone rang, but he didn't recognize the caller ID so he ignored it. It had been ringing a lot lately, but Gregory didn't want to talk to anyone. He wanted to win this damn game.

He picked up a piece of ham and pineapple pizza from the box, shook off the flies and reclaimed it as his own. He washed it down with a warm Coke; the kitchen and its fridge were just too far away. For a moment, Gregory looked around at his apartment in the real world. He saw the empty pizza boxes, Chinese food cartons and cans and cans of Coke and Mountain Dew. There were insects boldly wandering through the mess in the dim light coming through the blinds. As he watched, a large centipede crawled out of a soda can, its improbable number of legs twitching through the small opening. Gregory was repulsed, mostly by the bug, but also himself.

He shut out the real world and returned to the game. His Avatar was standing there, waiting for him patiently, occasionally tapping one foot or the other, looking around, shrugging or other small movements to keep the player from getting too bored.

"Okay, Blackstone," he said. "Let's do this thing." Gregory brought up the first of the four challenges and Blackstone tackled it with electronic vigor. It required both combat and strategy, which was the best kind; Blackstone rose to the occasion, a mighty warrior and Gregory's brain puzzled out the complicated riddles and they both moved past it. Three more and he could face the last Demon Lord at the end. He was pretty sure Blackstone would win that fight, and he was anxious to get to it.

Challenge #2 was easier than the first: purely physical and no problem for Blackstone. #3 was mostly word games, tricky and damnably time-consuming; after he finally puzzled them all out, he had to fight twenty-five Wargs at once. That was awesome.

Gregory noted that three hours had passed, and that he had to pee. He had been putting it off for over an hour, but if he didn't go now, he was going to wet his pants. He peeled himself off the couch and lurched to the bathroom. He let fly and it lasted over a full minute, turning the water in the stained bowl a pale yellow. Gregory looked in the mirror. It had been weeks since he shaved, days since his last shower. He tried to remember the last time he'd brushed his teeth, but could not. He breathed into his hands and sniffed. Yuck. He looked at his dry toothbrush and the tube of Aim next to it. He stood like that for several seconds, pants still unbuttoned and tried to summon the energy to care.

Someone knocked on his door. He froze and stared at his reflection. Nobody visited him. Ever. The knock came again, louder. Gregory wondered if they could hear the background music of the game. He hoped not; he didn't want company. Didn't want to talk to anyone. They knocked again, pounding on the door.

"Hello? Is anyone there? We heard someone is still living here. You have to leave. You have to get out of there! This building has been condemned and will be torn down tomorrow! Hello?" There was a pause, then Gregory could hear muffled voices outside his door, then footsteps retreating.

Tearing down the building? That's insane. He'd lived here his whole life. He hadn't left his apartment in... months? A year? He couldn't remember. After the accident at work, he'd had no reason to go anywhere. Never having to work again was a small price to pay for one little toe. Come to think of it, he had noticed it was quiet lately. He couldn't remember the last time he heard Old Lady Smothers' TV being played too loudly. But, he figured she had died; she was, like 106 or something. Maybe he was the only one here. Maybe they really were tearing down the building. Maybe he should have answered the door. But, they said it was happening tomorrow, so today was safe. He didn't have to leave yet. Gregory had plenty of time to finish his game.

Challenge #4 was hard: Blackstone had to solve a puzzle, perform a difficult acrobatic feat *and* defeat a solid opponent. It took him nine attempts to pull it off. That was awesome. Gregory released the mouse and did a little victory dance with his fingers, the only part of him that ever moved fast. He was vaguely aware of noises outside and looked at the window. He could see the sky getting lighter behind the blinds. It was morning already? He'd have to order breakfast soon; his stomach growled at the thought. After I beat this guy and win the game, Gregory decided. Then, I'll eat. Something else was nagging at him, too. Something about today. He couldn't remember.

On the screen, Blackstone faced the Demon Lord, drew his sword and shook his head, like "you ain't shit, buddy." Gregory's left hand flew across the keys and his right manipulated the mouse. He was in the zone. He and Blackstone were wearing down the Demon Lord, but Blackstone was getting pretty beaten up, too. It was epic, perfect. The graphics were amazing: you could count the Demon Lord's teeth as he threatened to bite Blackstone's face off.

Gregory was peripherally aware of a large diesel engine firing up outside. Some kind of heavy equipment. He knew this was important, but wasn't sure why.

Blackstone was bleeding from several fairly serious wounds, but the Demon Lord was hurting more. Both stood panting on the screen. They had been fighting continuously for almost 90 minutes and both were exhausted. Gregory had to admire the attention to detail the game designers put into this. The Demon Lord suddenly leaped for Blackstone, trying to take him off guard, but he was ready, dodging the claws and burying his sword deep in the thing's shoulder. The Demon Lord bellowed in pain as the sun went out behind the blinds. Gregory flicked his eyes in that direction; he was

174

loathe to take his eyes from the screen, but needing to know what was happening.

The sun was hiding behind an immense black wrecking ball on a thick chain. It smashed through his window and then blinds, taking out wood and drywall on either side. Time slowed down for Gregory. He watched individual shards of glass burst through the room, one of them stabbing him in the upper left arm, one missing his face by a quarter inch. The blinds, improbably remained attached to the wall, flipping up and rattling like tiny bones. Gregory could peripherally see the computer screen; Blackstone paused with his sword in the Demon Lord's shoulder. The Demon Lord, in Blackstone's moment of hesitation, clamped his mighty jaws over Blackstone's head, severing it from his body. Blood fountained upward on the screen. The wrecking ball smashed through his apartment, digging a furrow in the floor. It came for Gregory as if he had somehow done it wrong. His hands were still on the computer, still trying to finish the game when the ball hit him. On the screen, the Demon Lord bellowed in triumph as Blackstone's body fell at its feet. At that moment, Gregory's body was crushed into pulp; his mind had time for one last thought: *I probably should've gotten off the couch.*

Then oblivion.

KEN MACGREGOR

About the Author

Ken MacGregor's work has appeared in over fifty anthologies, magazines and podcasts. Ken is a member of The Great Lakes Association of Horror Writers and an Affiliate member of HWA. You can find Ken on Amazon, Goodreads, Facebook, and at ken-macgregor.com. Ken's the kind of guy that, if he found himself stranded somewhere with you, would probably eat you to survive. Ken hopes you enjoyed the stories in this collection and that you sleep just a little less well because of them. Ken lives in Michigan with his family and two unstable cats.

APPENDIX:

FIRST PUBLISHING CREDITS

'A Creature Stirring' - *What's that Scuttling Down my Chimney* (Prospective Journal 2012)

'SeaWolf' - *Dead Sea* (Cruentus Libri 2013)

'Killer Bagel' – *The Siren's Call Issue #5* (Sirens Call Publications 2012)

'Disaster Blanket' - *Erie Tales V* (Great Lakes Association of Horror Writers 2012)

'Bad Squirrel' – *The Siren's Call Issue #3* (Sirens Call Publications 2012)

'Zombie Ate My Girlfriend' - *A Quick Bite of Flesh* (Hazardous Press 2012)

'Havin' a Bad Day' - *A Quick Bite of Flesh* (Hazardous Press 2012)

'First Case of the Year' - *Body Electric* (2010)

'Obsessive Compulsive Soldier' - *Body Electric* (2010)

'First Person Shooter' – *The Sirens Call Issue #8* (Sirens Call Publications 2012)

'Lawn' - *Dark Dreams Podcast* (2013)

'Deadweight' - *For All Eternity* (Dark Opus Press 2012)

13015107R00107

Made in the USA
San Bernardino, CA
07 July 2014